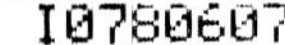

I0780607

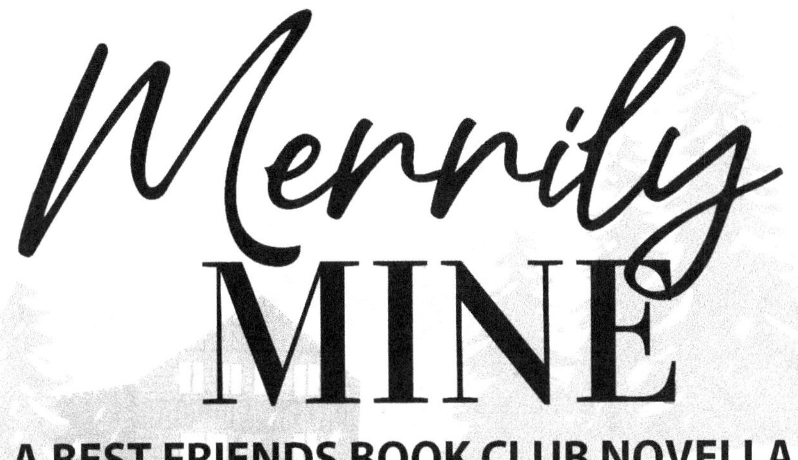

JENNIFER CHIPMAN

For the little girl who learned to ride horses in her pink cowgirl boots.
Never let anyone dull your sparkle.

playlist

- Starting Over - Chris Stapleton
- Back in the Saddle - Luke Combs
- All I Want for Christmas is a Cowboy - Megan Moroney
- Worst Way - Riley Green
- Landslide - Fleetwood Mac
- Am I Okay? - Megan Moroney
- cowboy like me - Taylor Swift
- Maybe This Christmas - Ron Sexsmith
- 'tis the damn season - Taylor Swift
- Jade Green - Kacey Musgraves
- Cold December Night - Michael Bublé
- Happen To Me - Russell Dickerson
- There Was This Girl - Riley Green
- When Did You Get Hot? - Sabrina Carpenter
- Neon Moon - Brooks & Dunn, Kacey Musgraves
- Baby, It's Cold Outside - Brett Eldredge, Meghan Trainor
- Almost (Sweet Music) - Hozier
- All I Want - Kodaline

- Before You - Benson Boone
- Christmas Tree Farm - Taylor Swift
- Bed Chem - Sabrina Carpenter
- Until I Found You - Stephen Sanchez
- How Do I Tell You? - Lizzy McAlpine
- invisible string - Taylor Swift
- you look like you love me - Ella Langley, Riley Green
- Would That I - Hozier
- Underneath the Tree - Kelly Clarkson
- Everywhere, Everything - Noah Khan, Gracie Abrams
- Would You Go With Me - Josh Turner
- If You Love Her - Forest Black
- weren't for the wind - Ella Langley
- Loving You On My Mind - Chris Stapleton
- Baggage - Kelsea Ballerini
- The Bones - Maren Morris, Hozier
- Beautiful Things - Benson Boone
- I'm Gonna Love You - Cody Johnson, Carrie Underwood
- All Your'n - Tyler Childers

Or scan below to listen to the Spotify Playlist:

1
emily

The world outside my window was a perfect blanket of white, coating the Montana landscape. It was a sight I was used to, growing up outside of Bozeman. Over the years, I'd decided there was nothing quite like a white Christmas. After years of traveling, it just felt like home.

Hence why I was here instead of a resort in the Maldives. They'd offered me a complete, expenses-paid stay for a few social media posts and some videos. *Why hadn't I taken them up on that again?*

Oh, right. *Snow.*

And maybe because I was just a little lonely.

Though part of me was regretting my decision to come home—mostly because my parents were looking at me with concern. As if I weren't a twenty-eight-year-old responsible adult, thank you *very* much. Like I couldn't take care of myself in their giant, eight thousand square foot house for the next two weeks. Because yes, I was spending Christmas completely alone.

"Your brothers aren't sure they're going to make it here

for Christmas this year. With the babies and all." My mom gave me a sad smile as she tucked her passport into her bag.

It felt like I knew what she was thinking. Poor little Emily —all alone for Christmas. Poor little Emily, the only sibling who hadn't found her person yet.

I loved my mom. And I knew she loved me. But sometimes, it was almost insufferable seeing the pity in her eyes. For her only daughter, who was close to thirty and had never even had a serious relationship in her life.

"Oh." My smile dropped. "Right. Of course." I hadn't been counting on it, but a pang of longing rippled through me, knowing my brothers were both happily married, with families of their own now. I enjoyed being an aunt—loved visiting Portland and spoiling my niece and nephews rotten —but the ache in my heart was always there. Wanting more. Wanting something for myself. Was that even possible now? What was the likelihood that I'd actually meet the one?

The older I got, the less it felt like a possibility.

It wasn't like I could just write a letter and leave it under the tree. *Santa, all I want for Christmas is a cowboy.*

I shook the thought away. Nope. I had to be content with my life; otherwise, I'd never make it through the day. I'd be too caught up with pining and loneliness to even function. Sometimes, it was almost crippling.

"Are you sure you'll be okay by yourself, Em?" my mother asked again, that concerned expression still on her face. "I can call—"

"No, I'll be fine, Mom," I said, hiding my emotions by tugging down the hem of my green slouchy sweater. "Besides, I'm a *big girl*." Resisting the urge to roll my eyes, I continued on. "It's not like I haven't traveled all over by myself. Don't worry about me—I can handle two weeks alone."

Clearly, they didn't seem to trust that I'd be alright, which was more upsetting than anything else. Sure, it was the first holiday I'd be spending by myself, but that didn't mean I couldn't handle it.

Normally, we'd all come home to Montana to spend the holidays together. Things had changed over the last few years, especially with both of my older brothers living in Oregon and me jet-setting around the world. I hadn't gone to college, but I had built up an incredibly successful social media platform. Being an influencer had perks, like having the closet of my childhood bedroom full of items brands had sent me, and traveling on someone else's dime. Even if it *was* a never-ending stream of fake smiles and staged photos on my perfectly curated feed.

Honestly, I was tired. That was the main reason I was home. Technically, I didn't have anywhere else to be. I didn't have an apartment of my own—I'd spent the last two months on a road trip across the country.

And since my parents had booked a two-week vacation to the Bahamas, I was the only Sullivan with no plans this year.

My dad ran his hands through his gray hair, wandering around the kitchen with a mug of coffee in his hand as my mom scurried about, finishing packing.

When had they gotten so old? Both of my parents were retired surgeons, and had been workaholics my whole life. It was strange to see them as doting grandparents who happily embraced life, all things they never had time to do when we were younger. It was hard to be resentful—I knew how much they loved us and worked hard to give us a good life.

"I always worry about you, hun. You're my baby." My mom came to stand in front of me, tugging on a strand of my hair. I looked like a combination of my brothers—same nose and chin as Benjamin, but with lighter brown hair and Hunter's green eyes. Did she see her two successful sons every time she looked at me? Did she wish I were more like them? "Especially when you're out seeing the world."

Wrapping my arms around her, I hugged my mom tight. "I know you do. I love you."

"Love you too, Emily." She squeezed me tighter. "I asked the neighbor's son to check in on you in case you need anything."

"*Mom*," I groaned. I didn't need babysitting. "Really? I'm almost twenty nine-years old." Which was basically almost thirty. I was really trying not to think about that.

She batted her eyes. *What was my mother up to?* I frowned at the thought. "Wait." The only neighbor near us who had a son was... "The neighbor's son? *Mason*? I thought he was living in Washington somewhere."

Not somewhere—*Seattle*. Happily married with his college sweetheart. It wasn't like I'd been keeping tabs on him specifically. His mom just loved to stop me whenever I was home and talk my ear off about her precious baby boy.

Okay, it was cute. Even if he was thirty-six.

"He moved back after the divorce," Mom said. "I'm surprised you didn't know."

Divorce? I blinked. "I wasn't gone *that* long, was I?" Did I somehow wake up in an alternate dimension? *And why was my heart racing just from hearing the news?*

She patted me on the shoulder. "Well, if you need anything, I'm sure he'd be happy to help."

An offer I wouldn't think about too much. "Thanks, Mom." I looked down at my watch. "What time do you need to leave for the airport?" I'd offered to take them, but they'd turned me down, citing icy roads. I hated driving when it iced over. There was a lot of snow in the weather forecast this week, and I planned to spend most of it curled up inside, watching old Christmas movies and drinking hot chocolate. *Was it too early to spike it?* I contemplated the thought. It was five o'clock somewhere, right?

My dad placed his mug in the sink, now empty, and came over to stand in front of us. "Our car is coming in ten minutes." He wrapped his arm around my mom's waist. "Assuming your mom is ready to go." Dad winked at me.

Mom rolled her eyes at him, patting him on the chest. "Of course I am, honey. Suitcases are packed and by the door."

He pressed a kiss on her cheek. "Then let our daughter be. She'll be just fine, sweetheart."

She sighed, taking a step towards the door before turning back to me. "The fridge is fully stocked, and I gave the housekeeper two weeks off, but if you need her—"

"Mom." This time, I laughed. "I can clean up after myself. It's fine. Stop panicking."

"You should have seen her in the OR," my dad grumbled. God, I could only imagine how amazing it would be to see her in the operating room, taking charge.

Not that I'd want to see anyone's insides—I was firmly *not* a fan of blood or other bodily fluids. There was a reason my older brother was the doctor of the three of us and not me.

I smirked. "Alright, you two. Go on your tropical vacation and have an amazing time. Soak up some sun for me." I wouldn't get any here. Not when the ground was already covered in a few inches of snow, and the Montana winter wouldn't be kind to me. Sure, I'd lived here my entire life, but in the last few years, I'd become somewhat of a wimp. I blamed all the time I spent in warmer climates. I wasn't above shoving my feet in a second pair of wool socks to keep them warm. "Have a pineapple drink for me," I said, all but pushing them out the door. "I'll be fine, I promise!"

After my parents were finally gone—one last hug and reassurance later—the house was empty.

Yeah, I was ready for my two weeks of silence. My content

was scheduled and all of my brand contracts were fulfilled, meaning all I had to do for the next two weeks was... *nothing*.

God, that sounded nice. Scratch what I said before—I was *seriously* glad I'd agreed to come home for Christmas.

My Kindle was loaded full of books, including the new one that my brother Benjamin's wife, Angelina, had illustrated the cover for. Both she and my other sister-in-law, Gabbi, were best friends with the author, Noelle Harper. I'd gotten to know her pretty well myself over the last six years since she'd been a bridesmaid at both of my brother's weddings. Which was how I'd become obsessed with her writing. I definitely was looking forward to getting lost in the new love story she'd written. Her heroes were always swoon-worthy, and that was more than I could say for the guys in my life. Was it so much to ask that I found a man like *that?*

At least I'd have my books to keep me company.

Sitting on the couch, I looked at the space where a tree normally sat. They hadn't put one up this year since they'd be gone, and I had to admit, the space felt a little lonely without the warm lights and presents underneath the tree. Not that I needed one just for me. It felt frivolous, especially when I'd already shot all my Christmas content earlier this week.

Pulling a blanket over my lap, I stared out the large picture windows that looked over our property. It was a beautiful winter day, with the sun high in the sky making the snow sparkle, and the pine trees standing tall past our pastures and horse barn.

The barn where my horse, Smokey, the beautiful dappled gray, waited for me. When I'd gotten back from my last trip, I promised myself—and her—that I'd start taking her out for daily rides again. Maybe the fresh air would be good for me. Help me figure out what was next.

After all, I never imagined I'd be twenty-eight and still single.

Dating apps were *useless*, and I'd given up on the idea of meeting someone in a bar or while traveling. Hookups might have been fun at first, but they'd never amounted to anything. And though my parents had offered to set me up— *multiple times,* might I add—with the single doctors that worked at their hospital, I'd always turned them down.

"Stop chasing the fairytale," I muttered out loud to myself. But was it so wrong that all I wanted was a man who was obsessed with me? One who wasn't just the love of my life, but also my best friend. Someone I could talk to for hours without getting bored, who would get down on his knees and worship me.

The last one might have been the romance novels talking, but damn, I missed sex. I missed *good* sex. And I certainly wouldn't find someone to hook up with at a bar in town. Not when the chances of running into someone I went to high school with were high. Or someone who knew my parents or my brothers, and…

Safe to say, the only orgasms I was going to be getting were battery powered ones. Though I wouldn't turn down the opportunity if it came knocking.

I sighed, smoothing a hand down my face. "You're a mess, Emily Sullivan. Nothing has changed. Of course, the perfect man wasn't waiting on your doorstep to sweep you off your feet. That kind of thing only happens in romance novels." I paused. "Or Hallmark movies."

Maybe I should adopt a dog. Especially if I was going to stop traveling all the time. I needed to get a place of my own and act like an actual adult, even though I had no clue what I was going to do with my life now. It wasn't like I had a *career.* Social media was all I knew. I was tired of influencing, but what else did I have? *Nothing.*

Snuggling up under my blanket, I opened my book on my Kindle, getting lost in the story of a witch falling in love with a wolf shifter. I'd already read a few chapters before my phone buzzed with a text from my best friend, Hannah. We'd become friends in middle school and had been glued at the hip ever since.

HANNAH

Hey! How's it going? You're back in town, right?

EMILY

Yep. Got back in yesterday. The parents left a few hours ago.

Wanna go out tonight? We can go to Giddy Up like old times.

I debated saying no—that I was too comfortable under my blanket on the couch and had no desire to move. But then I thought about all the things I wanted in the future. Things I couldn't have if I just sat at home by myself.

The idea of meeting a hot cowboy and letting loose.

You know what? Fuck it. Let's do it. I was just going to sit here in my pajamas and read, anyway.

What about the husband?

Eh, he's fine.

Besides, I've *earned* this, Em.

I laughed, just imagining my spitfire of a friend—who was happily married—telling the husband who doted on her she was going out and he didn't have a say.

In the meantime, I shoved my feet into my boots, heading out to the barn to give my pretty girl Smokey a few treats and take her on a short ride.

Later that evening, dressed in jeans that made my ass look *great*, plus my favorite pair of boots, and a black top that emphasized my cleavage, I walked into Giddy Up. It was our local cowboy-themed bar. They had line dancing nights every week, something we'd taken advantage of many times when we were younger.

The walls were decorated with various memorabilia—photos from the local rodeo, trophies, lassos and old spurs. Even a few cowboy hats graced the space.

Hannah waved to me from a high-top table, and I let out a sigh of relief.

"Em!!" She leapt up, wrapping her arms around me with a giant grin on her face. Her copper hair was in tight waves that hit below her shoulders, and she'd worn a cute long-sleeved off-the-shoulder top and dark jeans, with a pair of practical boots, her coat draped on the chair behind her.

"Hi." I hugged her back, grinning as we pulled apart. She'd been my best friend since forever. I still remembered when she'd moved to town and we'd immediately bonded. The two of us had always been close, even when she'd gone away to college and I'd somehow stumbled onto internet success after some of my content had gone viral.

It also didn't hurt that she never treated me like a spoiled rich girl like so many other kids in this town had. Obviously, my parents were well off—they were both top surgeons at the hospital—and the custom-built house we lived in was set on forty acres, but I didn't like it when people assumed I was just living off my parent's money.

After all, I had plenty of it saved up from all my brand deals over the last two years.

"God, I know I saw it all on Instagram, but I want to know *everything!* How was the trip? Is it weird being home now?"

I shrugged, sitting across from her. "Honestly, it feels like I haven't been home for two years." Though to be fair, I hadn't really. Besides a few days here and there, I'd had a suitcase packed and a flight booked. The last time I'd been here for any length of time had been for Hunter's wedding.

"You've missed *so* much," she said, her eyes growing wide.

Yeah, I really had.

Especially when it felt like everyone I'd grown up with was now married and had two point five kids and the perfect little family.

The question from earlier still lingered: *how had I gotten to twenty-eight still completely alone?*

And how had I missed that Mason Elliott was now divorced?

"Should we get a drink?" I asked, looking at the bar. "Or are you still nursing?" Getting a little happy drunk sounded like a *great* way to spend my first full day at home. Though it didn't exactly prove I was the responsible adult that I wanted my parents to see. One night wouldn't hurt, right?

She waved me off. "I can pump and dump. It's my first night away in *forever*. Anthony's got this."

Standing up, the two of us both walked to the bar, flagging down the bartender so we could order drinks—a whiskey sour for me, and a gin and tonic for her.

"How's it been? You know… being a mom?" I asked her, watching him make our drinks out of the corner of my eye. The nice thing about living in a town like this was even though it was small, and sometimes it felt like you couldn't even go to the grocery store without running into someone you knew—it was also big enough that I didn't know the bartender. Thank *God*.

Hannah let out a little sigh of happiness. "*Amazing*. I never knew I could love a little person this much. I mean, you were there. He was *so* tiny."

I grinned. "Yeah." There was no way I'd miss my best friend's baby shower or being there for her when she'd given birth. Hannah had clarified that I was *absolutely* getting disowned as godmother if I wasn't there. Luckily, the timing had worked out between brand trips. "I'm happy for you," I offered, an ache blooming in my chest.

It was hard to admit how desperate I was to find something like that for myself. Over the last few years, it had felt impossible. Sure, I'd dated, but my life hadn't exactly lent itself to a long-term partner.

"You'll find someone," she said, with more optimism in her voice than I could muster up.

Would I? It didn't feel like that anymore.

"I don't know." Looking down, I swirled the liquid in my glass. "Sometimes it feels like that's just not going to happen for me." I shook my head. "But it's okay, really. I have my niece and nephews." Benjamin and Angelina's twin boys were a year and a half now, while Hunter and Gabbi's daughter was eight months. "And my godson, of course." I beamed, thinking about her chubby-cheeked baby and how the top of his head smelled like heaven. "So, I'm fine. I'm the cool aunt, you know?" The one who would swoop in with presents before leaving for another exotic trip.

Except… why did that life feel empty now? Why did I feel so hollow inside?

"That's a lot of denial I hear there—" Hannah teased.

"Shut up," I muttered. I picked up my drink, taking a long sip, when I could literally feel the energy in the bar change.

Like all at once, everyone had quieted.

"Woah," I said, turning my head towards the door at the sight of two bulky, muscular cowboys who'd just entered. Thanks to the brims of their hats, I couldn't quite make out their faces. "Is that—?"

2
mason

iddy Up, the local cowboy bar, wasn't exactly my idea of a good time, but my buddy Jonah had asked me to get a beer, so here we were.

It had been over six months since I'd moved home, but sometimes it still felt like I was an outsider. I was back in Montana to stay. This was home. I loved it here—the way the air was crisp and fresh. The feeling of riding my horse across our property, with the air whipping through my hair. Being able to wear my hat and boots without the city girls looking at me funny.

After all, I'd been born and raised on the ranch. It was about time I took over from my parents. They were both getting older, and after the last ten years in Washington, it was good to be back.

Tugging my hat off, I ran my hand through my dark hair as I stared up at the old, shoddy exterior. Jonah, standing at my side, was wearing a pair of dark-wash jeans and a giant grin on his face.

"Remind me why we're here again?" I asked as he opened the door.

"We're getting a drink," he answered seriously.

I resisted rolling my eyes. Sure, I was thirty-six, but that didn't mean I couldn't find him completely ridiculous. "But why here? There's so many other bars in town." Bars that weren't full of tourists looking to score a real-life cowboy. I'd had enough of that at the ranch.

My friend grinned. "It's line dancing night."

That's when I realized the bar was *full* of women. Women who stared at us like we were their next meal. I groaned, turning back to my friend. "No."

"Yes." His look was downright roguish, and I knew he'd played me.

"Jonah—"

"It's been a year since your divorce was finalized, man. It's time to move on. Who knows, maybe you'll find a nice girl here tonight?"

"I need a beer," I muttered, moving over to the bar and waving down the bartender.

What I *didn't* need right now was a wingman. Or to find a woman.

I was perfectly content with my life the way it was. Even though sometimes I craved companionship and a warm body next to mine. Not that I'd ever admit it. I looked at my bare ring finger, where I could almost see the ghost of a ring. The reminder of my failed marriage. It had been a year since I'd taken it off, and yet I still felt the weight of it on my skin.

Fuck, I was a mess. I was still trying to get my head on straight.

After the bartender slid my drink over to me, I brought the glass to my mouth, taking a long pull.

My eye caught on a brunette leaning against the opposite end of the bar. Gorgeous curves. Long silky brunette hair that would look perfect wrapped around my fist. I couldn't see her face, but damn. She was talking to a redhead, holding an old-fashioned glass in her hand.

A girl with taste. I liked that.

But damn, this was so not what I needed right now.

"You should go say hi," Jonah said, smirking.

I pushed at his shoulder. "That defeats the purpose of celebrating being single, doesn't it?"

"Nah. You deserve a little fun."

Grumbling, I downed the rest of my beer. "Maybe I'm just not any fun anymore."

"That's bullshit, and you know it."

Jonah quirked an eyebrow. "Is it?"

Scrubbing my hand across my beard, I pondered that thought. Fun. "I haven't been with anyone since—"

"Since Maggie. I know."

God, was it that obvious? I sighed. "Fuck, man. I'm not ready for a relationship, and you know it."

"Now, who said anything about a *relationship*?" He gave me a shit-eating grin. "Just go say hi to the beautiful woman, Mace. Have fun, remember?"

"I don't know." I rolled my empty glass between my hands. "You sure? I don't want to ditch you."

"Yes, my man. *Go.* She's been looking over here and checking you out, too." My best friend grinned. "Show her you know how to show a lady a good time, alright?"

Fuck it. I could be fun. I could go flirt with the most gorgeous girl in this godforsaken bar and not think about tomorrow. For tonight, I could pretend I wasn't going home alone to an empty cabin. That my marriage hadn't failed, setting me back to square one at thirty-five years old.

My entire life, I'd had a plan for my future. Only now that I was here, closer to forty than I was to thirty, none of it had come true. Still, the ranch would be mine soon. That was something.

Maybe I'd wasted my youth on the wrong woman, but I wouldn't make that mistake again.

I adjusted the hat on my brow before sliding my thumbs into my front pockets. Was I really going to do this? Go over there and say… what? *Hi?*

What the fuck was I supposed to say? The last time I'd asked a girl out, I was in college.

Before I knew what I was doing, I was halfway across the bar. No turning back now. I could do this. I could be that guy again.

Sliding in behind her, I wrapped my hand over her waist, letting it rest on her hip as I dipped my head down to whisper in her ear. "Hey, gorgeous." She turned around, and —*"Fuck."*

I knew her. She wasn't just some brunette beauty in a bar —this was my childhood best friend's little sister. *Emily Sullivan.*

Little Emmie Sullivan.

Jesus, how could I not have recognized her? I stepped back, pulling my arm back, so I wasn't touching her. Still, the sensation fizzled from where my skin had brushed over hers, like there were actual sparks. It felt I was a goddamn high schooler all over again. "I didn't—"

"What, cowboy?" She cocked her head, fluttering her eyelashes. "Expecting someone else?"

It had been years since I'd seen her, and *goddamn.* Maybe that was why I was completely tongue-tied, standing in front of her like I couldn't remember my own name.

Her redheaded friend at her side laughed, whispered something in her ear, and then disappeared back towards a table.

"Hi, Em," I croaked. I didn't know what I expected seeing her for the first time after all these years, but it hadn't been this. The years had been good to her. She was a far cry from the shy little kid she was back when I was in high school and spent every day with Hunter.

Emily was nothing like I remembered. She was even more gorgeous up close, where I could appreciate every inch of her body. That silky brown hair that hung down her back. Her dark green eyes reminded me of Christmas trees. Her body, wrapped up in jeans that clung to every curve and a black top that showed off mouthwatering cleavage. Lips painted red as sin. Sultry eyes. Fuck.

All things I absolutely should not be noticing about Hunter's little sister. I shut my eyes. Damn. *Hunter*. We were best friends growing up, though we'd grown apart when we'd gone to different colleges. It was understandable, though. He'd gone to medical school and become a pediatric doctor, while I'd been perfectly happy staying at Montana State and getting a degree in Ranch Management.

After all, one day the Elliott horse ranch would be mine. Except… I'd met Maggie and had ended up in Washington. In the life I thought would fulfill me—would make me happy. But it hadn't. It had just left me bitter and resentful, and we wanted two different things.

She gave me a soft smile, twirling a brunette strand with her finger. "Hey, Mason. It's been, what, two years?"

"God, yeah." The last time I'd seen her had been at Hunter and Gabbi's wedding, though I hadn't really noticed her then. I'd spent most of the night fighting with Maggie. I'd seen the writing on the wall for months before the wedding, but that was when it had been over for me.

"Mom told me you moved back. I'm sorry to hear about the divorce." Emily ran her finger over the rim of her glass.

"I'm not," I admitted, reaching out to place my hand over hers before thinking better of it.

Touching her was bad. Touching her was definitely not something I should do.

She blinked. I wondered if she'd expected that from me—honesty. But I didn't regret getting a divorce. I didn't wish that things had worked out with my ex-wife anymore. She'd made her choice, and I'd made mine.

"Oh." Emily bit her lip. "I don't—" She let out a small laugh. "I guess I don't know what to say."

"You don't have to say anything." I shook my head, shoving my hands into my pockets. "It's in the past." I rubbed my empty ring finger. "Besides, I'm over it." The lie felt wrong, even on my tongue, but the more I said it, the more it would be true, right?

All I could do was move forward. I knew what I wanted, now more than ever. The ranch. A family. A life of love and laughter. Things we would never have together. I didn't blame her, but I'd long since stopped mourning the life I'd thought we would have.

"Well, in that case…" Her lips curled up. "Maybe we should start over."

"Oh, good. So we can forget about when I slid in here, thinking you were just a beautiful stranger in a bar and attempting to flirt with you?"

"Is that what we're calling it?" Her eyes sparkled with mischief. "Oh, I'm definitely never going to forget about that, cowboy." There was something about the way she said the word, about her eyes landing on my hat, that made me want to be bold. Want to embrace whatever this was, going on between us.

I shrugged, taking a drink of my beer. "Well, it was worth a shot."

"So, you think I'm beautiful, huh?" She twirled a strand of hair around her finger.

It was hard to deny. "You own a mirror, don't you, darlin'?"

What was I thinking? She was eight years younger than I

was, and totally fucking off-limits. I shouldn't be telling her how pretty she looked tonight, how she took my breath away the moment I saw her across the room.

Hunter would kill me, wouldn't he? This was his little sister. His baby sister.

And yet, there was no way I could pull myself away from her.

Her green eyes connected with mine, and we both laughed. It felt good to laugh with another person—to feel like, if only for a moment, I could let myself be free.

"It's good to see you, Mason." She smiled.

"You too, Emily." There was a glow to her skin—a warmth that made her practically glow in this dimly lit, grungy bar. "Haven't seen you around much," I said. Not that I'd spent many nights out since I'd moved back. Most of the time, I had a date with my bed after working the ranch all day and then woke up before the sun rose each morning.

She fidgeted with the charm bracelet on her left wrist. "Yeah, I've been traveling a lot. I've been back here and there —mostly to visit Hannah." She nodded towards where her friend was sitting at the table, texting on her phone. She was vaguely familiar, though I assumed it was because they'd probably spent time at the Sullivan house when Hunter and I used to goof around after classes. "I've been spending a lot of time in Portland, too." Emily tucked a piece of hair behind her ear.

"Visiting your brothers?" I guessed.

She nodded. "They've always been in such different places in their lives—that happens when you're so much younger—but now... I don't know. Both of them are *so* happy. Wives and babies and all that." She waved her hand in the air. "And I'm just..."

"Stuck," I answered for her. God, it felt like she was

prying the word from my soul. We were in different situations, and yet…

"Exactly. Not that I don't love my job, but… I guess I figured I'd have my life figured out by now." Emily frowned. "I don't know why I just told you that." She stared down at her empty glass.

I chuckled. "Maybe we should get another round of drinks?" I looked across the bar at Jonah, who was chatting with two girls, a blonde and a dark-haired duo. He was fine.

She nodded, and I waved over the bartender and ordered us both another drink. "On me," I insisted.

"Thank you," she murmured.

I raised my glass after he set both down in front of us. "Of course. My pleasure." Emily clinked hers against mine. "Cheers," I said, taking a sip.

She hummed. "What are we celebrating?"

"Old friends?"

Emily rolled her eyes. "We were never *friends*, Mason." She looked away. "Back then, I was nothing more than your best friend's annoying kid sister. I was practically invisible."

I frowned. Maybe she'd been younger than Hunt and me, but I'd never minded when she tagged along with us. "Maybe we weren't friends *then*. But that doesn't mean we can't be friends now." I winked at her.

She pursed her lips as if she were debating the idea.

"Is the thought of being friends with me really so bad?" I placed my hand over my heart. "I'm hurt, Emmie girl."

Her cheeks turned pink, and she looked away—*bashful.* This was the Emily I remembered: quiet and always blushing around me.

Not the vixen of a woman in front of me, the one who looked like temptation and *sin.*

The totally off-limits gorgeous girl who I definitely wasn't allowed to want.

3

emily

*E*mmie Girl. There was something about my childhood nickname on his tongue that really did me in. *Who was the man in front of me, and what had he done with Mason Elliott?* Never in my wildest dreams had I ever pictured him *flirting* with *me*.

Friends? Could we really be *friends*? My heart sped up, beating faster as I took him in. The way he filled out those Wranglers. His green plaid flannel that almost seemed to bulge around his muscles. Even his damn boots and the brown leather jacket he was wearing. I swallowed roughly.

Because this man was every wet dream come to life. And it was *so* unfair. Because he was Mason. My brother's best friend growing up. The boy I'd watched at every opportunity. Riding horses, playing video games with my brother, or hanging out in the living room with my family.

The cowboy I'd been crushing on since I knew what a crush was.

Is the thought of being friends with me really so bad? No, no, it wasn't. And that was the problem.

Because I was just like everyone else. I was pretty sure

20

every girl within a twenty-mile radius had drooled over him when he was younger. He was stupidly attractive, and damn if he didn't know it. Cocky as all hell, and definitely not for me.

"No," I finally answered him. "No, I don't think it would be so bad at all."

I reached up, stealing his hat off his head and placing it on mine, fluttering my eyelashes.

His eyes filled with heat, and his eyes raked over mine, not even trying to hide his attraction to me. I liked that. The blatant perusal, the way he'd been so bold earlier, sliding in and wrapping his arm around my body.

Mason stepped forward, the stubble on his cheek brushing against my face as he dropped his mouth to my ear. "You know what they say, darlin'."

"Hm?" I tipped my head back, pressing up onto my tiptoes. It was the first time I could really appreciate how tall he was—how he seemed to tower over me with that impressive height and build. There was no denying how Mason spent his days, not when he looked like *that*.

He flicked the brim of the hat up, exposing my face to the light.

Mason's head dipped low, his lips only inches from mine. "If you wear the hat, you gotta ride the cowboy." His voice scraped over my skin, making goosebumps appear on my arms.

He couldn't be… *no*. "Is that so?" My voice was all breathy. Damn if I didn't know it. I was just pretending to act coy, hoping he wouldn't see how much he affected me.

There was no way that Mason was thinking about what it would be like to be with me, right?

Of course not. Except… He hummed against my skin, taking the hat back and placing it back on his head.

My body felt like it was on fire.

Fuck, he was hot. Hotter than he had any right to be. I'd done my best to forget that fact over the last ten years—namely because he'd never seen me as anything other than a kid growing up—and then because he'd been married. He was taken. Off-limits.

And now, he was… *what?*

Divorced. Living in Montana again. My neighbor.

Even so, he was… Mason. My brother's childhood best friend. The man who was *good*. Who rescued kittens from trees and talked in soft voices to his horses. The man who never failed to make me smile growing up. Who would share his cookie with me—Hunter's kid sister and all. Who put a bandaid on my cuts and scrapes I'd gotten when I'd followed them around.

My heart was racing.

I let my eyes drift down to his empty ring finger. The gold band he'd worn the last time I saw him at Hunter's wedding was gone.

It's in the past, he'd said. *I'm over it.* And yet, there was a darkness that seemed to cling to him, something behind those blue eyes that seemed to say the opposite.

Suddenly, I wanted to take that darkness away from him.

Maybe he was just as lonely as I was.

Maybe being home didn't have to be so bad.

His eyes dipped from my eyes to my mouth, and then back up. What would it be like to have his mouth on mine? To have that beard scraping against my skin as his tongue gently pushed inside—not asking for permission, because Mason might have been a gentleman, but he would take what he wanted. And I'd give it to him gladly.

"Mason, I—" I swiped my tongue over my lips. Drank the rest of my drink in one gulp, as if it would give me the courage to say the words desperate to spring free. I… *what?* What was I about to say? About to do?

Something stupid like asking him to kiss me. God, maybe I'd had too much to drink. I definitely had, if I was thinking of something insane like that.

Turning my head, I looked at Hannah over my shoulder. She raised her eyebrow, the question obvious on her face. We'd always had an unspoken language between us, and I knew what she was asking. *Do you need a rescue?* I gave a small shake of my head. This was Mason. I was perfectly safe with him. No matter what I said, no matter what happened between us, I had no reason to doubt that.

"I should go," Mason said, setting his empty glass down on the bar.

"What?" I turned back to look at him, a frown filling my face. "But I thought…" I'd thought we were having a good time. *Fun.* Wasn't that what we were saying? "You don't want to stay a little longer?"

He shook his head. "Have an early mornin' at the barn. You know how it is. Especially with the weather the way it is." Mason took off his hat, running his fingers through his hair before replacing it again. "You…" He cleared his throat. "You have a safe way home tonight, Em?" No more Emmie Girl, I guess. We were back to Em. Still, I liked how he was worried about me, that he wanted to make sure I'd be okay. The ten-year-old who had doodled his name on all of her notebooks was practically jumping for joy. I tried to remind that girl that we weren't infatuated with this cowboy in front of us anymore—that at twenty-eight, we had moved on from the silly childhood crush, but it was hard.

Harder still, with the way he was looking at me with concern in those deep blue eyes.

I nodded. "Yeah. Hannah's husband is going to pick us up." That was why I'd taken an Uber to the bar earlier.

"Good." He rubbed his hand over his beard.

I wondered what it would feel like on my skin. Between my thighs.

Down, girl, I scolded myself. Damn, I was being a horny bitch. Turns out all it took was one cowboy in a Stenson and Wrangler jeans for my body to come back to life.

"Night, Emily."

"Goodnight, Mason," I whispered, watching him walk out the door, hands shoved inside his jean pockets. He said something to his friend and then slipped outside.

Fuck it. I ordered another drink. Alcohol was needed, especially after I'd just been rejected. Somehow, he'd anticipated what I was going to ask and had taken off before I could ask it. *Dammit.*

Hannah frowned as I slid back into my seat at our table. "What just happened? You two looked like you were having a good time."

"Thought we were." I turned and looked at the door where he'd just disappeared outside. "Honestly, I have no idea, Han." Propping my elbow on the table, I rested my head on my hand. "He just…" I shrugged, twirling my straw around my drink.

Was it crazy to think maybe I could have a bit of *fun* over the next two weeks while I was home? Maybe. But it was even crazier that I'd actually thought about suggesting it to Mason. Of course he'd turn me down. Of course he didn't want to *kiss me.*

I groaned. "Let's never speak about this again."

My head was pounding, and I was seriously questioning my last drink I'd had before we'd left the bar last night. I was getting too old for this. Letting out a groan, I buried my face into one of the soft, plush pillows that littered the living room couch.

Why did I drink so much? I rubbed my temples. The smart thing to do after being rejected by my much older brother's childhood best friend would have been to go home and hide, to let the sting of embarrassment fade. I hadn't done that. Somehow, I was even more mortified this morning.

Running my index finger over my lips, I thought about that moment when his eyes had found my mouth. *Was I really going to ask him to kiss me?*

I'd been so sure he was interested in kissing *me*, too.

But then he'd bolted.

The doorbell ringing startled me out of my thoughts.

I looked down at my outfit, trying to decide if I was respectable enough to open the door. I'd pulled on a cozy snowflake sweater, a pair of leggings, and giant slipper socks this morning. At least I was *clothed* and not in my pajamas. Honestly, I considered that a win in my book.

It was like my mind was playing tricks on me, because there was a tall, muscular cowboy waiting. He had one hand propping himself up on the doorway and the other perched on his hip. *Hot damn.* That shouldn't be attractive. But it was.

There was a cowboy hat on his head—a different one— and he was wearing a red plaid shirt underneath a thick Carhartt jacket with a pair of jeans and work boots.

"Hi," I squeaked out, remembering to say something finally.

His blue eyes sparkled in the mid-morning sun as he stood up straight. "Hey, Emmie Girl."

I winced. My childhood nickname was a reminder that he was eight years older than me, and he'd never seen me as anything other than a kid. As my brother's little sister. He'd made that clear last night.

"I just wanted to make sure you were doin' okay."

"You didn't need to come check on me," I insisted, hand still clutching the door. "I'm fine. My mom's a little overbearing, but she should really know that I can take care of myself."

He just blinked at me. "What?"

I frowned. "Didn't my mom send you over here to make sure I was okay?"

Mason raised an eyebrow. "No. I mean, she told my mom you were staying here alone, and asked if I could help if you needed anything."

Yeah, that sounded like Mom. "I'm not a kid anymore," I grumbled. "I don't need to be checked in on."

His voice was deep when he muttered, "*Clearly,*" under his breath. Like I couldn't hear him.

I didn't move from my spot inside the door, though I regretted not bringing the blanket from the couch with me. It was chilly outside, and I shivered, even in my sweater.

"Did you need something, or was that it?" I asked, cocking an eyebrow. "Because I'm letting out all the warm air, cowboy."

"*Emily.*" The commanding tone in his voice made me shudder, but it wasn't an unpleasant feeling. No, it was the opposite. *Did he have any idea how hot he was?* God. I shouldn't be thirsting over him. That horny bitch from last night was rearing her ugly head.

"Mason." I crossed my arms over my chest. I really needed to get laid. Maybe then I'd stop thinking about him like that.

He sighed, rubbing his forehead with his pointer finger and thumb. "Can we start over?"

I hesitated for a moment. "Sure…?"

"I wanted to come check on you after last night. I know I…" He cursed under his breath. "Leavin' like that was an asshole thing to do. I'm sorry."

My breath caught in my throat. "Oh."

Mason nodded. "So, I just thought I'd say hi. See how you were doin'."

Biting my lip, I shivered, and then looked between him and the warm inside. "Do you want to come inside, maybe? I can make you a cup of hot cocoa."

"Sure." He smiled, following me in towards the kitchen.

I was trying to remember to breathe. After all, in all the years that I'd crushed on Mason Elliott—all the years of my innocent infatuation with my brother's best friend—we'd never been completely alone like this.

"You don't have a tree?" Mason said, looking around the living room as I started pulling what I needed out of the giant pantry. The house was open concept, so the kitchen and living room shared one large space.

I shook my head. "No. Mom didn't see any reason to put up the trees when she, and I quote, *wouldn't be here to enjoy them*." I sighed. Never mind that *I* would have enjoyed them.

Mason furrowed his brow, like the idea had never even occurred to him.

Normally, my mom would decorate with a twenty-foot tree in the foyer and a smaller tree in the living room where we hung all of our family decorations. This year, the only decorations in the house were our family's knit stockings hanging on the fireplace. There was a new addition this year, since Hunter's daughter had been born this spring. Mom had added a new stocking for her.

Thankfully, the mantle was big enough to support their growing families. Would I ever have one of my own? My stocking felt so lonely up there without a matching pair.

"Here you go," I said, sliding a mug across the counter after I finished making two steaming cups of hot liquid.

He inhaled deeply before letting out a hum of appreciation. "Mmm. That's the good stuff."

I tried to ignore the warmth that bloomed on my cheeks as I watched him drink it, his tongue darting out over his upper lip to gather a dollop of whipped cream that had landed in his mustache.

"About last night…" I started, wringing my hands out. "I'm sorry if I crossed a line or made you uncomfortable. You're Hunter's friend, and I shouldn't have—"

His eyes darted up to meet mine in surprise. "You didn't." Mason's words interrupted mine before I could even finish my thought. "I promise, Emily."

"Still." I couldn't hold back my blush.

He took his hat off, setting it on the counter so he could run his hands through his hair. "Last night, I…" He shook his head. "I needed to leave before I did something stupid."

"But what if I *wanted* you to do something stupid?" I sipped my hot chocolate slowly, looking up at him over the rim. The giant island kept us separate, but suddenly, the room felt too small and my clothes too tight.

"Emily." His voice was low.

I waved him off. "It's really okay. You don't have to make excuses for me, Mason. I'm a big girl; I can handle myself. I saddle my horse and everything."

Just because my family was wealthy, and I was spoiled doesn't mean I didn't know how to do things myself. I resented the fact that people thought that. Sure, I'd gotten lucky with my content going viral on social media apps, which had allowed me to build up my platform, but creating it wasn't just a walk in the park. It had taken a lot of hard work, a lot of persistence. A lot of videos went nowhere before I built up my brand.

He frowned. "What's that supposed to mean?"

If he didn't know, I didn't want to have to explain. "Never mind. You should probably go. I'm sure you have a lot to do at the ranch, tending to the horses."

"Tell me." It wasn't a request—but a command. The words scraped over my skin.

"What do you want me to say, Mason? That everyone has treated me like a princess my whole life? That I'm almost thirty years old and I've never had an actual job and sometimes it feels like I just…" I shrugged. "I don't need one more person who feels the need to tiptoe around my emotions. I'm not delicate."

Mason's face was full of so much emotion—the same concern from last night, but something else, too. Something I didn't quite know how to translate.

"What fuckers have been telling you this?" He sounded… angry. But that couldn't be right.

Everyone, I wanted to say. *No one.* I let my eyes drift shut for only a second. *Myself.*

I looked away. "It doesn't matter." Because it didn't. My voice was soft when I finally spoke again. "My point is, you don't have to handle me with kid gloves. I won't break."

He picked up his hat, setting it on his head before tugging at the brim. "I know you won't break, darlin'. You're as strong as steel. Always have been." He walked towards the front door. "And Emily?" His deep voice called out as I watched him turn around to look at me once more.

"Hm?"

"Don't listen to them. They don't know anything."

I swallowed roughly. "Okay." The word was a whisper.

And then, he was gone. But for whatever reason, his words stayed with me for the rest of the day.

It would be a long, long time before I could get them out of my mind.

4

mason

I shouldn't be looking at her like this. Shouldn't be wondering what it would be like to kiss my best friend's little sister.

But *fuck.* Even without a lick of makeup and wearing leggings and an oversized sweater, she'd been stunning. I'd never noticed how beautiful she was before last night. How alluring her very presence was.

She wasn't the girl I remembered. At the wedding, I'd been too tied up with Maggie to notice her. Now, I couldn't hold back.

But what if I wanted you to do something stupid? Goddamn. Her voice had been all breathy, and for a moment I'd almost caved. Gave in to the spark of attraction between us. It was hard to deny. This was why I'd left the damn bar last night. She'd been looking at me with those big green eyes, and I knew what was going to happen next. We'd dance. I'd give in to the fantasy of tasting her lips. We'd go back to my place, spend all night in bed together, and then—*what?*

She was too sweet. Too young for me. And yet, I'd shown up at her house today to check on her, like I needed to lay eyes on her to know she was okay. That Emily wasn't upset after the way I'd brushed her off last night before she could say whatever she had wanted to.

And I had. She was fine.

Emily made it clear she could take care of herself, so why was I still standing on her porch? Why—after I'd finished that cup of hot chocolate that tasted like heaven in a cup, rich, creamy and covered in whipped cream—could I not bring myself to walk back out to my truck?

I had things to do today. The ranch wouldn't run itself. Midnight Pines Ranch was my family's legacy—my parents' pride and joy—and I'd be damned if I let the place fall apart under my leadership. I wanted to bring it fully into the twenty-first century, to finish modernizing our equipment and update the guest cabins that brought in most of our revenue over the year, including during the winter when the tourists came for things like sleigh rides and horseback rides in the snow.

The holidays on the ranch had always been my favorite time of year. I'd enjoyed coming home every winter, getting to see the ranch during Christmas. Even back then, I'd wished I were here more. Now that I'd moved back, I wasn't taking it for granted. I was going to enjoy every bit of my first Christmas back.

I looked up at the sky. There was a laundry list of things I had to do before it started snowing again tonight. I'd heard on the radio that we had a snow advisory for tonight—they were expecting another two to four inches to fall overnight. Thankfully, it wasn't enough to *significantly* affect the area since we were used to heavy snowfalls. There were enough snowplows in the area that the probability of getting snowed in was low. It happened, though, especially when a freak snowstorm hit.

Grumbling, I finally made my feet move, wrenching my

truck door open and climbing back inside, turning up the heater as I drove back to my family's farm. It wasn't too long before I was driving under the wooden archway that was hand-carved with the Midnight Pines logo, a horse standing in front of three pine trees with a crescent moon overhead.

Home. It was such a powerful feeling, knowing I was exactly where I was meant to be.

Sure, I missed parts of my life in Washington, but I didn't miss the job. More than anything, I missed the ease that came with my life there. I missed having someone to fall asleep next to, someone to hold and to be there when life got hard. The biggest change after the divorce was getting used to being alone again.

I'd never imagined having to start over in my mid-thirties, but here I was. Single, alone, and living in the old A-frame timber cabin on our property. Over the summer, I'd worked relentlessly to fix it up, spending every second I wasn't working on the ranch on refinishing the floors, repainting the walls, and redoing almost every surface in the place. Now, it looked brand new. It was small, but it was mine. *Completely* mine.

When we'd divorced, Maggie and I had sold our house, splitting the profits from the sale between us equally. Luckily, we didn't have too many assets and hadn't had kids, so the entire process wasn't too painful. Even though it had felt like a scab that kept getting picked at before it could heal over. Sometimes, I felt like I could still feel the scar on my heart. In the last year, I hadn't even recognized the woman I'd fallen in love with in college. Maybe we were just too young—or maybe we were never meant to last.

I wished her the best, even as I tried not to mourn the time we'd spent together. The years I'd lost and could never get back.

Instead, I looked towards the future. The future of Midnight Pines Ranch, that was.

My future… I ran my hand down my beard, trying to ignore the ache in my heart. Sure, I'd love to meet the right person and get married again. To have the kids I desperately wanted. When I closed my eyes, I could picture it: a large farmhouse with a wraparound porch, with little brunette kids running around in overalls and cowboy boots, their hair in pigtails tied with bows. But that didn't mean it would *happen*.

And I'd have to be okay with that.

Snowflakes fell as I headed off to the stables.

And for just a moment, I paused, letting myself take it all in: the beauty of the Montana landscape as it became covered in a blanket of soft white. The dark green of the pines, the mountains in the distance, the crisp smell of fresh snow in the air.

No matter what happened, I resolved not to take advantage of this view—not for one moment of the rest of my life.

"Hey there, boy." I patted the neck of my horse, Whiskey, as I entered his stall. "Thought you might like to go for a ride." He let out a short whinny, his ears flicking forward.

I grabbed a comb, running it through his coat, letting my mind calm as I focused on grooming him. Every step came naturally to me. I'd been taking care of horses since I was little. Growing up on a horse ranch meant I'd had my own practically since I could walk.

He was a Thoroughbred with a gorgeous coat that had reminded me of the color of whiskey—hence his name.

We'd missed our ride with everything I'd been up to yesterday once I got back from the Sullivans', including a mound of paperwork that had been waiting for me in the office. With all the proposed updates to our guest cabins on-site, it had taken me longer than expected to go through it all.

Today, I was going to make up for that. There was a fresh coating of snow on the ground—it had continued throughout the night—but thankfully it had stayed soft, not turning into ice. We could keep operating the rides as long as the weather remained favorable, which our guests definitely preferred.

I'd flicked on the radio before I came into the stall, and I listened as the weather report came over the speaker. *"There is a winter storm watch in effect for Gallatin County from midnight tonight to midnight Monday. Expect six to eight inches of snow accompanied by a chance of ice. Roads and bridges will likely become slick and hazardous. Consider delaying all travel. If travel is absolutely necessary, drive with extreme caution…"*

"That doesn't sound good," I muttered to myself, already thinking about what we'd need to do if the watch turned into a *warning*. Send the staff who didn't live on the property home, first. Our guests would be fine in their cabins, and our cook—my mom—lived in the main house. Part of us staying open year-round meant the ranch hands were trained for extreme weather and these sorts of things.

When I finished brushing Whiskey down and had cleaned his hooves, I turned to grab his saddle and pad, finding the ranch's foreman walking into the barn.

"Hey, Mason." Benson pulled off his gloves, tucking them into his coat pocket as he headed towards me. Dad had hired him a few years back, when he'd been getting older and ready to retire from the more hands-on aspects of managing the ranch. He was in charge of day-to-day operations on site, and I was grateful to have him, especially as I re-acclimated to being here. I couldn't imagine trying to run this place and all of its many facets without him.

I dipped my head in acknowledgement. "How's it going, Benson?"

"You getting ready to take Whiskey out?" He was wearing a thick jacket over his normal attire of jeans and a flannel shirt. In the winter, I often ended up layering, since some of the heavier lifting meant we'd get overheated quickly.

My horse let out a small snort. He grinned, pulling out a handful of sugar cubes and feeding them to my greedy creature. "I'll take that as a yes."

I draped the blanket over his back, making sure it was in the right place before grabbing the saddle. "Figured I'd take him out for a quick ride since we missed yesterday. The snow's not too bad right now. Sounds like it's going to be worse tomorrow, and the horses will all be cooped up if the ice is too bad."

Benson winced, rubbing his hand down Whiskey's muzzle. "It sounds like it could be pretty bad. I've already got the guys prepping."

I let out a sigh of relief, knowing he had it under control. "What would I do without ya?"

He slapped my back. "Luckily, you don't have to worry about that. You're stuck with me, Mase. Midnight Pines is my home." Benson Sterling started here at eighteen, though he'd grown up in the Bozeman area. "You know I love your momma." She'd taught him how to ride a horse as a kid. Back in the day, she'd been one of the best horse trainers in the area, and though she'd hung up her stirrups years ago, I still loved watching her ride.

"Thanks, man."

He nodded, running his fingers over his mustache. "I'll let you go. Enjoy your ride. Check in when you get back, alright?"

"Sounds good. Don't work too hard." I frowned, looking outside. "If the weather gets worse, I don't want you working out there in it."

The man just patted his chest pocket. "Don't worry, boss, I'm dressed warm."

I resisted rolling my eyes. "Not your boss yet." Technically, my parents still owned the ranch, even though everyone knew I'd come home and was in the process of learning the ropes to take over.

This was my legacy. Everything I'd ever wanted. And now it was so close, I could almost taste it.

He shrugged. "Soon enough, you will be. We all know the place is in expert hands under your leadership. I've seen how hard you've worked in the last year since moving home."

Reaching back, I scratched the back of my head, feeling a sudden rush of emotion. "Thanks. I really appreciate you sayin' that."

He dipped his hat, then strolled out of the barn, back into the winter wonderland of the outside, and I returned my attention to my horse.

"Ready to ride?" I asked him, as if I expected an actual answer, and finished saddling him, making sure it sat level and properly behind his shoulders. After he was all fastened up, I gave myself a nod. *Let's do this.*

Putting one foot in the stirrup, I slung my other leg over my horse, mounting him quickly before rubbing at his neck. Squeezing my legs, I clucked my tongue, and then we were off.

Whiskey barely needed any guidance or prompting. Not when he knew the trails by heart. We'd been riding them together since the day I claimed him as my own.

One day, maybe, I'd have a partner at my side, riding a horse of her own. But for now, I was fine being alone.

Hours later, I sat in my office, working on my computer, watching the snow fall. Whiskey was back in his stall, happily munching on his dinner when I'd left him, and I was happy to have gotten some time in with my horse.

Especially because... Fuck, it was coming down real hard outside.

My thoughts drifted to Emily, all alone in that giant house. Would she be okay? Was she prepared for the storm? She was so different from what I remembered, and yet... in so many ways, the same. Her eyes still twinkled with delight. When she was warming up to someone, she was quiet, and then after that she would never shut up. But I'd never minded when she talked my ear off.

I resisted pulling out my phone to scroll through her Instagram account for the third time today. Something she'd said yesterday wasn't sitting right with me. Like people judged her for what she'd chosen to do. I might not have understood it, but I could tell that she put a lot of hours into her work. I didn't like the idea that someone could dismiss her so easily.

"Did you hear?" Benson popped his head into my office, distracting me. Probably good, because I'd already pulled my phone out of my pocket and was about to open the damn app up again.

"Hm?" I perked my head up. "Hear what?"

He grimaced. "The storm got upgraded to a winter storm warning. It's going to be bad. I'm trying to get everything ready before I head back to the bunkhouse."

"Oh, fuck." My first thought was Emily. And then I cleared my head. Focused on the problem at hand. The ranch. That was my responsibility, my focus. "Do you need my help with anything?"

Benson shook his head. "No. But your momma mentioned

something about checking in on the neighbor's daughter? Said you should go over there since she's all alone."

Fuck. Of course, Mom would send me over there. I'd mentioned that I'd run into her at the bar the other night, though I hadn't told her I'd found her stunning. I smoothed a hand over my face.

Somehow, she knew it anyway.

He raised an eyebrow at my lack of response. "What's that about?"

"She's just meddling," I explained, rolling my eyes. This was just like her. I'd lost count of how many women she'd introduced me to since moving home.

"Well, she's probably right—if she's really alone, go make sure she's ready. She has horses too?"

I nodded. They didn't have a ranch, but they had their own stable, and I could just picture Emily going out to the barn in a blizzard. *Dammit.* Had she seen the warning? I didn't even have her phone number to text her and make sure she knew.

Without another thought, I shot out of my chair, rushing over and grabbing my coat.

Guess I was heading to the Sullivan house.

5
emily

Emily, this might be the dumbest shit you've ever done," I muttered to myself, tightening my arms around my waist as I headed back to the house. Well—*hopefully*. I felt like I could barely see in front of me, hoping I was at least going in the right direction. The snow was coming down thick—thick enough that I could barely see. Plus, I hadn't grabbed my snow boots, which had better traction. I hadn't even grabbed my jacket, just running out to check on Smokey without thinking it through fully.

She was fine, though I could tell the high winds battering against the sides of the barn had made her extra skittish. I tried to soothe her, talking in a low, calm voice while stroking her muzzle and neck. Once she was calm enough, I filled her food, swapped out her water, and put a blanket on her. I was grateful the stable was structurally sound and heated—my parents had spared no expense—so I didn't have to worry about my horse if the snow continued to get worse.

My foot hit a patch of ice, and I slipped, ending up on my ass. "Ouch." I winced, rubbing my back. I'd gone down *hard*. Damn. That was going to leave a bruise. To make things even worse, the cold and wet from the snow had already started soaking into my jeans.

A concerned voice had me looking up in surprise. "Jesus, Em, are you okay?"

Oh.

Oh, God. I looked hopelessly at the ground. *Why now? Why* did he have to see me like this? Damn, this was mortifying.

Because Mason Elliott was standing over me, all bundled up, with a beanie pulled over his head and somehow still looking like the sexiest man I'd ever seen, and I was sitting in the snowbank in whatever I'd thrown on this morning.

Shivering, I rubbed my hands up my arms. "I'll be fine. Just—" My teeth started chattering as I tried to stand up, but slipped again. "Fuck."

Mason, without skipping a beat, pulled the beanie off his head, shoving it over mine before scooping me up into his arms. "I've got you, darlin'."

"I can walk," I insisted, even though he'd just seen me look like a baby deer who didn't know how to use her legs. Which… fair.

He ignored my words of protest. "Come on. We need to get you inside." I tried to ignore how it felt to be cradled against his body like this. One of his arms was under my legs, the other supporting my back. "Hold on." He looked at me until I wrapped my arms around his neck, and I looked away, hoping the cold had already made my nose and cheeks pink enough that he wouldn't be able to see me blush. Mason looked up at the sky. "It's getting worse out here."

"I know." I looked at the ground, the layer of snow already piling up higher. My whole body shivered again, and I did my best not to bury my face in Mason's jacket as he navigated us back towards the house.

"Did you miss the weather announcement?"

I shook my head. "Yes?" I winced.

"Dammit, Emily." He sounded… angry. "It's a winter storm warning. You shouldn't be outside."

I felt small. "I'm sorry." My voice was quiet, barely able to be heard over the roar of the wind.

He let out a huff, but didn't say anything else, stomping through the fresh snow as I pressed tighter against him, hoping to steal more of his body heat. Snowflakes were clinging to his hair and eyelashes, and I resisted the urge to brush them off.

When we got to the covered back porch, he set me back on my feet—though he didn't move away from me, enough that I could still feel his heat at my back as I let us back into the house.

I was wet and cold, and all I wanted was to go get warm. Maybe take a hot bath, and then curl up under blankets.

When I turned around, there was fire in his eyes. "What were you fucking thinking, Darlin'? You could have gotten seriously hurt. If I hadn't been there, what would have happened?"

I crossed my arms over my chest. "I don't need to be treated like a child, Mason."

"Maybe you do."

Narrowing my eyes, I gave him my best glare. "Fuck this," I said. "I'm tired of everyone treating me like I can't do anything. Like I'm not twenty-eight years old."

Mason grit his teeth. "You didn't even put on a *jacket*. And where are your fucking boots?" He looked down at the shoes I'd slipped on in the house, figuring it would be a quick trip to the barn and back to check on Smokey.

Knowing he wouldn't like the answer, I didn't deign him with an answer. They weren't the best choice of footwear, obviously. And my sweater was warm, but not that warm. I was still shivering, even inside my heated house. Obviously,

I'd been out there longer than I'd originally meant to be, and the storm had been much worse on the way back.

"You're freezing," he said simply. All I could do was nod. Mason let out a curse. "Fuck. We need to warm you up."

My eyes widened. "W-*we*?"

"I—" He swallowed roughly. "You. *You* need to warm up."

My cheeks flushed, and I turned, not wanting him to see the dirty thoughts in my mind. Why was I suddenly thinking of the ways we could keep each other warm? About him peeling off my wet clothes and using his own body heat to warm up mine?

"I'll go—" I started. I'd go, *what?* My brain was suddenly empty. Like I couldn't for the life of me think of any actions I could perform. "Um." I turned to look at Mason.

His eyes locked on mine. "Take your clothes off, Emily."

Oh my God. The command scraped over my skin, and I could feel my peaked nipples in my bra. Under other circumstances, I'd imagined him saying those same words to me.

"Oh, right. Right." I babbled, reaching for the hem of my sweater.

Mason let out a strangled sound. "What are you doing? Not *here*."

Fuck me. What *was* I doing? About to get naked in front of Mason Elliott, because that suddenly seemed like a good idea?

Without another word, I scurried down the stairs to my room, quickly peeled off my wet clothes and dropped them in a pile on my bathroom floor. Grabbing clean underwear and soft, cozy pajama bottoms to pull on, I dressed just as fast. Not bothering with a bra, I slipped on an oversized crewneck sweatshirt.

It was the farthest thing from my wardrobe on Instagram,

to the person I portrayed to the outside world, but I didn't care. This was Mason, after all.

Shivers still wracked my body, so I grabbed a plush pair of socks and a blanket. I still had his hat, and for whatever reason, I didn't want to take it off my head. Wrapping the blanket around my shoulders like a cape, I trudged back upstairs, surprised to find Mason rooting around the kitchen.

"You're still here," I breathed out as I watched his shoulders flex underneath his long-sleeved henley. While I'd been changing, he'd taken off his coat, leaving it draped over the back of a barstool, his boots by the door.

Mason turned his torso to give me a small smile. "You thought I'd leave you after that?"

I didn't know *what* I thought. But having company was surprisingly nice. "I don't know. I'm still trying to figure out why you're even *here*, Mason." There were only a few reasons he would be, so I was trying not to look too deeply into any of them.

He kept his back to me, continuing whatever he was doing, not making eye contact as he murmured, "I came to check on you."

I shut my eyes, letting out a deep breath. "Didn't we go over this earlier?"

Mason didn't respond. I cracked open an eyelid, finding him standing in front of me, a steaming mug in his hand. He held it out to me, and I frowned. "What is this?"

"Hot chocolate." He raised an eyebrow, as if that should have been obvious. And it was. But that wasn't what I was asking, and I was pretty sure he knew it. "To help you get warm."

Taking the mug, I wrapped my hands around it, already feeling better. "I wasn't even outside that long," I muttered, looking outside. The entire world outside was *white*, as if the entire landscape was swallowed by the snow, though the sky was growing darker by the minute.

He just watched me as I sipped on the drink, feeling my body grow warm. Though I wasn't sure if it was from the hot chocolate, or the way he was looking at me. Letting the blanket drop to the floor, I set the mug down on the table next to me.

Took a step, and then another, until I was standing right in front of him, toe to toe.

My heart thumped in my chest, a pounding melody that sought an answer. "*Why?*" I asked again.

He knew what I meant. "You know why, Emily." He balled his hands into fists at his sides, his blue eyes locked on mine.

"I need to hear it." Needed to hear him say the words.

Why he'd left the bar. Why he was so insistent on checking on me. Why I felt the way I did.

"There's a winter storm warning." He repeated the same words from outside, as if that made a difference.

My tongue swiped out over my bottom lip. "*And?*"

"And..." He blinked. "You're all alone here." Mason frowned, like that meant something. And maybe it did. Maybe it meant everything.

"Mason... I don't understand. You rejected *me*." My words were a whisper.

He winced, shaking his head. "That's not what happened, Darlin'."

"No?" Because that was what I remembered.

Mason shook his head, running his fingers through his dark brown strands. "No. Told you I was trying not to do something stupid."

I propped my hands on my hips. "Right. And now... you're here, sweeping me off my feet, telling me you came to make sure that I was okay because I'm alone during a storm? So what *now*?"

"Fuck it." He let out a growl, stepping forward and swiping his beanie off my head before cupping my jaw. "I'm not sure I care anymore."

My eyes widened as his body pressed up against mine, eliminating every inch of space between us. His eyes were on my lips, and I swiped my tongue out, moistening them.

"You feel this—this thing between us—too, don't you? This... *heat*." He pressed his forehead against mine, still holding my face in his hands.

I nodded. Of course I did. I'd never been this attracted to anyone before. I was practically burning up with desire, with need. So much so that I didn't feel cold anymore. "But what does that change?" I asked him, feeling like I was ruining it before we even started. "I'm still Hunter's little sister." And I couldn't have that ruin things between them.

As much as I wanted this—wanted *him,* and had forever, I didn't want to be something he regretted. Because I knew, deep in my soul, that I'd never regret him.

His thumb stroked over my face, an intimate motion that made me practically pant in his arms.

"Mason..." I murmured.

"I want to kiss you. God know that I shouldn't, but I can't fucking help it, Emily. Is that what you want to hear? That from the very first moment I saw you in the bar two nights ago, you've been all I could think about?"

"*Yes,*" I said, letting out a gasp as his lips pressed against my neck, pressing soft kisses to my skin. "Please."

"Please, what?" Mason asked, moving his face until his lips were posed over mine.

"Please, kiss me."

He groaned. "Fuck. I thought you'd never ask." His arm wound around my body, every soft curve of my body snug against the hard planes of his. I was on my tiptoes as he bent down, and I appreciated how well we fit together, how he was practically sheltering my body with his.

And then—Mason Elliott kissed *me.*

Soft lips pressed against mine, tender presses of our mouths against each other. His beard rubbed against my cheeks as he peppered my lips and face with kisses before returning to my mouth. The time for delicate explorations was over. Our mouths opened, and we practically devoured each other. I wrapped my arms around his neck, digging my fingers into his hair, needing something to keep me anchored in this moment.

My eyes fluttered shut as his fingers dipped between the hem of my sweatshirt, fingers brushing over my bare skin. I let out a soft moan as his tongue met mine, stroking over and over, working me higher. I grabbed the back of his shirt, tugging on it and trying to free it from his pants.

"Emily," he groaned.

"You said you'd warm me up," I reminded him, pressing a kiss to his jaw and then trailing down his neck, appreciating the way his beard felt against my skin. "Remember?"

"God, you're going to kill me." He slid his hands up further, and I knew he was about to find out that I hadn't put a bra back on. Mason let out a sharp exhale of breath as he reached my bare back, thumb brushing over my spine.

The lights flickered, and then—the house went dark. The entire room plunged into darkness, dimly lit only from the last traces of light outside.

His voice dropped to a whisper. "*Fuck.* I think the storm might have knocked out the power lines."

I groaned, letting my head drop against his chest.

He pressed a kiss to my forehead. "Do you guys still have the generator?"

"Yeah." I nodded.

"Okay. I'll go check on it and see if I can get it running, and then I'll start a fire in the fireplace." He looked pointedly at me. "You stay in here and do *not* go outside."

Still a little drunk from that kiss, I didn't bother arguing with him. Instead, I plopped on the couch in the living room, swiping my finger over my tingling lips, trying to figure out if that had actually happened.

Was I hallucinating, or was Mason actually here? Maybe I'd hit my head when I fell on the ice outside.

Because that was the only thing I could think of to explain that he *wanted me too*.

6
mason

After locating the generator and making sure it was on —powering the stable's heater and the house, I headed back inside, finding Emily curled up in a ball on the couch, her eyes shut and her breathing soft. I left most of the lights off in the house, wanting to preserve energy, and instead used the flashlight of my camera to find a few candles and a lighter, illuminating the room.

I watched her for a few moments, seeing her chest rising and falling, appreciating the sight of her pink lips.

Part of me couldn't believe I was here. That I'd actually kissed her.

But she looked like she'd needed to be kissed, and who was I to turn her down? An idiot, that was who. Because after tasting her mouth, I couldn't believe I hadn't kissed her at the bar the other night. I should have asked her to dance. Twirled her on that floor, seen her cheeks blush with happiness, and then asked her if I could kiss her—the way a gentleman was.

But I wasn't a gentleman. And I was a little rusty at the whole dating thing. It had been years since I'd tried, and I didn't know what I was doing, clearly.

Pulling out my phone, I checked to see if I could get a message out to my parents, but it looked like whatever knocked out the power lines had also taken out the cell tower. There was no way I was getting home tonight. The storm roared outside, and my beard felt frozen after only a few minutes when I'd gone to check on the generator. Thankfully, the Sullivans hadn't skimped on the equipment, and after I'd heard the humming of the electricity flowing through it, I'd headed back inside.

Back to Emily.

I looked at the pile of wood that sat by the fireplace. I'd always loved their giant mantel in the family room, complete with a wood-burning fireplace. It wasn't often that there was a fire going in it, but during the holidays—and their annual Christmas party—it had always been going, making it feel extra cozy and homey.

She finally stirred after the fire was roaring, embers crackling and warmth flooding into the room. I'd spread a blanket in front of the fireplace, lounging on it, tilting my head back and enjoying the feeling of the fire on my face.

Emily rubbed her eyes, letting out a yawn. "Sorry. I didn't even realize I'd fallen asleep."

"It's fine," I reassured her. "You looked like you needed it."

She made a humming sound, stretching her arms over her head.

"Come here." I opened my arms, spreading my legs for her. Selfishly, after our kiss, I just wanted to hold her. I ignored all the reasons my brain told me it was a bad idea.

She blushed. "What?"

"We have to keep each other warm."

"Isn't that… you know, the point of the fireplace?" Emily pointed to the fire.

I smirked. "Sure is, darlin'. Doesn't mean I don't wanna hold you."

She crawled off the couch, leaving her blanket behind, and padded over towards me, a shy expression on her face.

Emily settled down next to me, and I shook my head. "That's not your seat," I insisted, pointing to my lap.

She worried her lower lip into her mouth. "Mason, I can't…"

Ignoring her protest, I wrapped an arm around her waist, pulling her onto my lap until her back was pressed against my front. I kept my arm over her stomach, keeping her pinned against me. "Better," I murmured against her ear.

Her breathing was rough, but after a few minutes, she melted against me, the fire quickly warming me up all the way through. Emily might have been able to change into dry clothes, but I didn't have any others with me.

I'd gotten in my truck, thankful that I had four-wheel drive and studded tires, and driven over here so fast I hadn't even stopped to think about grabbing anything. There was probably a duffle bag with a spare change of clothes or two in my backseat—I always kept them in there, in case of emergencies—but I wasn't trekking outside in the snow again to go find out.

Especially not when I had her in my lap.

This beautiful girl, one I hadn't been able to get out of my mind since the bar. Part of me wished she had just been some random stranger, one I could have flirted with and taken home to my bed, but Emily deserved better than just one night.

I pressed a kiss to her neck. "Now where were we…" I whispered, sliding my hands under her sweatshirt. Imagine my surprise when I'd realized she wasn't wearing anything under it. My cock twitched in my jeans at the thought of her rosy tits bare underneath the fabric.

She let out a gasp as I snaked my hands up her body, cupping her breasts and running my fingers over her nipples.

Emily arched her head back, turning to look at me.

"Yes?" I asked, pausing my efforts to make sure she wanted this.

She nodded. "*Fuck,* yes. Please touch me."

That was the only answer I needed—the permission to touch her like I'd wanted to for days. I massaged her breasts, rubbing her peaked nipples over and over. She let out a small moan, and I reached down, needing her sweatshirt *off.*

"I need to see you," I said, my voice hardly more than a rough rasp against her skin.

The sweatshirt came off, and then her creamy, bare skin was exposed to me. I pressed a kiss to her shoulder, ignoring my hardening erection.

Emily turned in my lap, giving me a full view of her pretty pink nipples for the first time, and I almost groaned. They were perfect, perky little handfuls that I wanted to get my mouth on immediately.

Fuck, she was gorgeous. "*God,* look at you." I shook my head. She was perfect. Undeniably beautiful.

How was a girl like her still single? How had no one scooped her up and locked her down? They were all damn fools. Emily Sullivan was like something out of a dream.

She made a humming noise as her hands trailed down my chest, tugging my henley out of my jeans before she guided it off over my head, exposing my chest.

"Look at me?" She tsk'd her tongue. "Look at *you,* cowboy." Her fingers traced the ridges of my stomach, over my abs and through my chest hair. Emily leaned forward, her chest pressing against mine as she wound her arms around my neck.

"Fuck it," I muttered, tracing my finger over her bottom lip. So sweet. So perfect. She smelled like cranberries and something sweet and *sin*. I couldn't get enough of it. Fuck holding back. Fuck staying away.

Her lips found mine once again, and it was a lazy exploration of each other's mouths as I dipped my fingers into the waistband of her pajama bottoms, sliding my thumbs underneath the elastic of her panties. *Fuck.* She bit my lip, and I kissed her back roughly, sucking on her tongue, needing *more*.

I left a trail of kisses down her neck before bending down to take her nipple into my mouth as she let her head fall back. Swirling my tongue over her hardened peak, I took my time to worship her breasts.

Emily whimpered. "Mason…" She rocked her hips, grinding down on top of my length.

Popping off her breast with a wet sound, I looked up at her, grinning. "*Goddamn*, darlin'."

Her breaths were coming out in little pants as she resumed her exploration of my body with her hands, letting them wander down to the bulge in my pants. She cupped it, squeezing lightly, and it was my turn to bite her lip.

"Careful," I warned, placing my hand over hers to still her.

"Or what?" She fluttered her eyelashes, and I grabbed her hips before rolling us, setting her on her back on the blanket.

Kissing her neck, I let my lips trail down her body, pressing them to the swells of her breasts, her stomach, before leaning back on my knees, resting my hands on her hips.

"Or…" I hooked my thumbs into the elastic waistband of her pajamas, dragging them down her skin before pulling them off her ankles. "I'm not going to be able to control myself."

Her brown hair spread around her on the blanket, and she ran her teeth over her bottom lip as I threw her bottoms off to the side.

"So do it. Lose control." Her voice was all breathy and low.

I ran my nose up the side of her leg. "Yeah?"

"Mhm." She took a sharp inhale of breath when I kissed her inner thigh. "*Yes.*" Emily nodded, giving me permission to continue.

Not hesitating for even a second, I pulled her panties down, sliding them off of her body until she was bare for me. A light dusting of brown curls covered her mound, and a blush covered her cheeks as I inspected her, unable to peel my eyes away from her alluring body.

Fuck, she was beautiful like this, all spread out on the blanket, one hand resting on her sternum and the other clutching the fabric at her side. Her brown hair was wavier than normal, after getting wet and then drying again, and her green eyes practically sparkled in the firelight.

"I need to taste you, right fucking now," I groaned as she spread her legs apart, parting those thighs for me. Giving me my first look at her pretty pink pussy, glistening and ready for me.

It was all the invitation I needed. Positioning myself between her legs, I dropped my mouth to her entrance, getting my first taste of her.

"Oh, *fuck*, Mason," she cried as I ran my tongue up her slit. But I didn't stop there—no. I lapped at her slit, drinking in her arousal. Flattening my tongue, I relished the feeling of having her under my mercy, whimpering with each flick of my tongue.

"So wet, baby," I groaned against her sweet cunt. She was *soaked*, dripping juices that I happily gathered with my tongue.

God, she tasted like heaven. I couldn't explain why the first swallow of her arousal felt *life-changing*, but it did. Like I would never be the same now that I knew what it was like to have my tongue buried inside Emily Sullivan's pussy.

Maybe I wouldn't.

Maybe something had changed forever when I walked up to her at that bar. I just hadn't known it yet. How my entire life would rearrange, how all of my thoughts would be filled with her.

I slid a finger inside of her, feeling her clench around me as I circled her clit, making her arch her back in pleasure, before sucking it into my mouth. She reached down, burying her fingers in my hair, as if she could force me in deeper, harder.

I could feel her getting closer to an orgasm, and I placed my second hand over her stomach, pressing down lightly as I worked a second finger inside of her. Fuck, I was so hard. It felt like I could come in my pants like a goddamn teenager just from eating her out. Feasting on her like she were the most delicious meal I'd ever had. *Goddamn.* I wouldn't last long.

But I needed her to come. Needed to feel her clenching around me, to have her come all over my fingers.

Pumping my fingers in her harder, I sucked at her clit, and a small cry slipped from her lips.

"That's it," I hummed against her clit. "Come for me. Soak my beard with your cum, darlin'."

"*Ohmygod,*" she cried. "*Mason.* I'm so close, I—"

She detonated, coming on a cry, her insides convulsing around my fingers. I couldn't stop myself from working her through it, fucking her with my fingers as I pressed down on her abdomen, licking up every drop that leaked from her pussy.

She collapsed back onto the blanket, panting roughly, draping her arm over her eyes as her chest rose and fell rapidly. "I've never—" She sucked in a lungful of air. "It's never been like that before."

Emily let out a small whimper as I pulled my fingers out of her, before sucking them into my mouth and cleaning off her taste from my skin. Her breath caught as I groaned at the flavor on my tongue, reaching down to squeeze my cock through the denim. *Fuck.* My cock throbbed in my jeans. Had I ever been this hard before? I didn't think so.

I propped myself up on my arms, climbing above her and caging her in. "It hasn't for me, either," I admitted. She was so beautiful like this, a light dusting of pink all over her body, perfectly flushed from my ministrations.

Her eyes widened. "But…"

Dropping a soft kiss on her lips, I shook my head. "I don't want to talk about anyone else right now," I said, kissing her harder, letting her taste herself on my tongue. She moaned as my tongue stroked over hers, squirming underneath me, and I tried to ignore my dick aching, desperate to be inside of her.

Down, boy. No way I was losing my manners now. I knew how to treat a girl, and Emily deserved to be treated *right.*

Adjusting our positions until we were face to face on the blanket, I pulled her into me. "Are you warm now?" I asked, running my hands up her ribs.

"Mmm." She arched her back like a cat, stretching out and pushing her nipples towards me. Fuck me, I wanted to put my mouth on them all over again. To cup those perfect handfuls. "Very warm."

"Good." I kissed her forehead. "Mission accomplished."

She let out a weak laugh. "Thank you." Her green eyes blinked up at me, and for a second, it was easy to ignore how my erection pressed against the zipper of my jeans, because she took my breath away. "I still don't know why you're here," she admitted.

For you. I ignored the question, reaching out to cup her

face. "You're so beautiful," I told her instead. She shut her eyes as I caressed her cheek, unable to keep my hands off of her. "So young. So sweet. So totally off-limits."

"No one has to know," she whispered, reaching for the button of my jeans. I placed my hand over hers, stilling her. "I… I want you." Her eyes connected with mine. That deep shade of green, like the forest pines outside, had me in a trance.

How could I tell her no? I couldn't.

"Emily," I groaned as she pushed the button out of the hole, unzipping my pants and shoving them and my boxers down until my cock sprang free.

Fuck. Me. Emily was a little vixen. One I hadn't expected, not one bit.

Her eyes widened as she took me in. "Do you think it'll fit?" Her hand wrapped around my length, and she darted her head down, running her tongue over the tip, licking off the pre-cum. "I want this inside me." She looked at me as she took me into her mouth.

"*Fuck*, Em," I groaned, thrusting a hand into her hair as she tried to take me in deeper. "I'm going to come way too fast if you do that."

Pulling off, she fluttered her eyelashes. "Do you not want to?"

I cursed. How did I explain why I was about to be the equivalent of a fumbling virgin who couldn't last? I couldn't remember the last time I'd been turned on. "I do, it's just…"

"It's been a while for me," Emily blushed, like she could read my thoughts. "I haven't slept with anyone in months."

I cleared my throat. "Same. It's been…" I grimaced. Even before the divorce, my ex-wife and I had been growing apart. It had been a while since we'd slept together, where I felt like I was sleeping in my bed next to a stranger. Shutting my eyes, I shook away the thought. I didn't want to think about her right now. Not with this beautiful woman in front of me, practically begging to suck my cock.

"Hey." Her voice was soft. "It's okay."

I opened my eyes to find her looking at me with so much care, so much compassion, that my heart nearly burst out of my chest. There was no pity there, however. Just pure desire. When was the last time someone had looked at me like this?

Sweeping her up into my arms, I lifted her into the air as I stood off the floor. "If we're doing this, Em, I'm not fucking you for the first time on the floor."

She wrapped her arms around my neck, pressing a kiss to my throat, sucking my skin into her mouth.

Fuck. There was no way I was going to last.

7
emily

*B*edroom?" he asked, practically panting as I pulled my lips off of his neck. God, the sounds he made when I had my mouth on him only made me want to do it *more*.

His cock was trapped between us as I wrapped my legs around his back, clinging to him like a koala as he carried me. It was heaven being in his arms. Burying my face in his neck, I inhaled his woodsy scent. It was heady and delicious, and I couldn't believe that for tonight, this beautiful man was *mine*.

I nodded, barely able to recognize the needy, wanton creature I'd become. "Downstairs. I'm in the basement." It was a daylight basement, so I wasn't surrounded by darkness, plus it gave me privacy that I wouldn't have had in my childhood bedroom.

He groaned, tightening his grip on my ass as he made his way towards the stairs. Every step made my sensitive clit rub against his erection, and I had to hold back my moans. It would be so easy to wiggle my hips, to position him just right so his tip slipped inside me.

I shimmied slightly when his arms tightened around me, crushing me further against him.

"Fuck," he groaned, pushing me against the wall and kissing me roughly, practically inhaling my mouth before pulling back. "You're a damn vixen, Darlin'."

I smiled at him, placing one of my hands on his biceps. "Not too bad yourself, cowboy."

He nipped at my ear as I thrust my fingers into his hair, every step down the stairs like a glorious version of torture and pleasure all wrapped up in one. I was so wet, so turned on, and all I wanted to do was slide up and down on his beautiful cock. It felt so good pressed against me like this, huge and throbbing, and I could only imagine how much better it would feel inside.

Scratching my fingers through his scalp, I kissed at his bare skin again, my hardened nipples pressed against his hard chest that was covered in a dusting of dark brown hair. *Hot.* Had I ever been this attracted to chest hair before? I didn't think so, but on him, it was all masculine, so freaking delicious. He smelled even better, if that was possible. Like juniper and pine and just a hint of lavender, his cologne made me want to bury my face in his flannel and inhale *deeply*. This mountain of a man, and right now… he was mine. All mine.

Mason opened my bedroom door, dumping my naked form onto my bed before kicking his jeans off. His boxers followed close behind. I sat up on my knees, watching him as he stroked his cock.

I licked my lips.

He took a step towards the bed.

"I knew you'd be big," I murmured, reaching out and running my fingernail up his length. It was my first thought the moment I'd seen him earlier. My second had been that I wanted to taste him.

"Fuck, Em," he rasped, body shuddering as he squeezed

the base of his erection. "You can't just say things like that." He was like velvet steel, so hard that I wondered if it hurt.

There was more pre-cum on the tip, and I wanted to lap it up again, to have his salty taste on my tongue. But Mason didn't give me a chance to take him back in my mouth, pushing me back onto the bed so my head hit the pillow. Using his knees, he spread my legs apart and positioned himself between my thighs, looking like a *god,* here for one purpose. To *fuck.*

"God." I ran my fingers up his washboard abs as I watched him work his cock. "Your body is unfair."

He grinned, still keeping up that lazy fisting of his dick.

I whimpered. "Please, Mason. I want you."

"You want my cock, huh, darlin'?"

I nodded.

He groaned, dragging the tip through my entrance, gathering up my wetness and coating himself in it. Every time he hit my clit, my back practically arched off the bed. "Condom?" Mason asked.

That made me pause, the haze of need diluting slightly. "I don't—*fuck.*" Shaking my head, I sat up. "I don't have any." Damn. And I *really* wanted him inside me.

After all these years of wondering, he was *here.* Wanting *me.*

Mason dropped his head onto my shoulder and pressed a kiss to my skin. "It's okay. We don't have to."

I bit my lip. "I'm… I'm on birth control. And I had an appointment a few months ago, so I'm all good. If you want to…"

"Are you askin' me to fuck you bare, Emily? Because…" He swallowed roughly, running his hands up my sides, squeezing my hips. "*Fuck.*"

Yes. "I want to feel you." I squirmed a little, his tip still notched at my entrance, wanting it inside of me.

"I'm good, too," he confirmed. "Had an appointment after the divorce was finalized, and I haven't been with anyone else."

The way he said it made me think she was the *only* woman he'd ever been with, and the thought made me want to make this even better for him. *Special*, somehow.

"You know, I've never had anyone inside me bare," I said, splaying my hand over my stomach. "You'll be the first."

"Are you asking me to fill you up, Emily?" His voice was deep. A rasp over my skin, like gravel.

I nodded, letting out a small whine as his head bumped against my clit again. "Please. I want to feel you. All of you."

"Goddamn. I won't last very long once I have this hot, wet cunt wrapped around me." He reached down, rubbing his thumb over my clit before rocking his hips, just the tip entering me.

I gasped as he pushed further into my entrance, stretching me out. He really *was* big. "You're not going to fit," I whimpered.

He groaned, stilling. "You're so tight." His hands gripped my thighs, pulling me apart. "So wet."

Looking down, I saw I'd only taken the first few inches. "*Mason*," I cried. There was something about his hot, hard length piercing me that felt even better than normal.

"Shhhh." He covered my mouth with his, kissing me deeply, every brush of his tongue against mine making me open up for him, relaxing my body. "Breathe."

Finally, when I was squirming, wiggling my hips once again, he pushed in farther, giving me more of his hard length as my body struggled to adjust to his size.

And then he started to *move.* Shallow thrusts at first, but each one brought him deeper inside me. "I know you can take more, darlin'," he grunted, snapping his hips in another thrust. "Take all of me."

His eyes were focused on the spot where his cock disappeared into my pussy, the sight so erotic I nearly came just from it. Not to mention the way he called me darlin', with so much devotion in his voice. Like he really wanted to worship me.

"I'm so full," I told him, placing my hand over my stomach and pressing down slightly, feeling the way he was buried tight in my body, every thrust hitting against my cervix. Wet sounds filled the room as he pounded into me, proof of exactly how turned on I was.

Was I really going to orgasm from this? Penetration *never* did it for me. Most of the time, I'd had to use a vibrator to finish myself off, because the guy I was with didn't put my pleasure first.

Mason wasn't like that, though.

"Come for me," he encouraged, grabbing my leg and adjusting us so he could drive in even deeper. "I want to feel you milk my cock before I fill that sweet pussy up with my cum."

Oh. Oh, he was filthy. I cried out his name as he bottomed out, the dirty talk making me even wetter. In and out, in and out, every snap of his hips driving me higher. "Mason, I need *more*," I whimpered. "Harder. Don't stop. Right there."

As if he were reading my mind, he brought his thumb to my clit, rubbing it in circles, reminding me of the way it had felt to have his tongue there, circling it over and over.

Cupping my breasts, I flicked my thumbs over my nipples before pinching them as he pistoned inside of me.

And then—"Yessssss," I mewled as my orgasm crashed over me. *Bliss.* My pussy spasmed around Mason's cock, fluttering sensations as he continued his shallow thrusts.

Mason groaned, dropping my leg and wrapping his body around mine. "*Fuuuck.* I'm gonna come."

"Inside me," I begged him, wrapping my legs around his back and forcing him in deeper, if that was even possible.

A few thrusts later, I could feel his cock hardening further, hard as steel, and his body tightening around mine. He grunted, letting out a curse as he spilled inside of me, a warmth that flowed inside my body.

He kept thrusting as he came, fucking his cum deeper inside of me. I groaned. "Mason. That feels…" I shut my eyes, not having the words.

Mason wrapped me up in his arms, rolling us onto our sides while keeping his half-hard cock still buried inside of me.

He brushed a strand of curly hair off my forehead. "How are you feeling?"

I sighed happily. "Perfect. God, I needed that."

My limbs felt languid, my body sore in all the best ways as I stretched my arms over my head. Mason pulled out, his cum dripping down my thigh, and I didn't think I missed the way the heat flared in his eyes as he watched it.

Still, we were both a little messy. I wrinkled my nose. "We should probably clean up."

He laughed. "There's the Emily I remembered." I stuck my tongue out at him. "You always hated being dirty, didn't you?"

I let my fingers trail up his torso. "Maybe I like it when *you* get me dirty, Mason."

He pulled me back against his body, his already hardening cock pressing against my hip as he pressed his head in between my breasts, letting out a guttural sound. "You're going to kill me."

Mason pressed a kiss to my sternum before hooking his arms under my legs and back, lifting me up out of the bed and carrying me to my en-suite bathroom.

"What are you doing?" I asked as he set me down on the counter.

He gave me a pointed look. "Takin' care of you."

I blushed. "Oh."

"Pretty good setup you've got down here." He changed the subject, looking around the bathroom as he turned on the shower with the flick of his wrist.

I responded with a hum. "I have privacy, at least."

"Don't tell me that." Mason closed his eyes.

"Why?"

"Because," my cowboy started. "I'll start getting ideas that I have no business having."

I wanted to hear more about those ideas, but he didn't give me a chance. Mason just helped me down off the counter before interlocking our fingers, guiding me into the shower.

Was it strange that in twenty-eight years I'd never showered with a man before? I turned to look up at Mason as the stream of water from my waterfall shower ran over us both. His blue eyes were bright as they seemed to take in my body, and I finally got to do the same to him. He towered over me, shielding me from the water with all of his muscles. Not a single inch of him lacked definition. God, he was beautiful. I bit my lip, letting my eyes drift lower. I still couldn't believe that had been inside me. He was definitely the biggest I'd ever been with, and fuck if he didn't know it. And he knew how to use it.

Reaching around me, he grabbed my body wash, squirting out a generous amount between his palms. I expected him to wash himself, but then his hands were on me, cleaning my body, rubbing over my my thighs and dipping inside my pussy. I let out a strangled sound as his thumb glided over my clit, and he smirked before washing himself. Something about him using my soap, smelling the same thing as me… it felt more intimate than what we'd just shared. A few days ago, he'd all but rejected me at the bar, and now we'd seen each other's *everything*.

But I couldn't delude myself into thinking this meant more. He might have been my first crush, but I wasn't naïve enough to think that this meant we'd be together now.

Definitely not.

So I was just going to enjoy it while it lasted, however long that was.

When we finished in the shower—though Mason did most of the work, making sure I was clean and then wrapping me up in a towel and drying me off.

I pulled my damp hair back into a braid after running my comb through it and using my typical hair products. Normally, I straightened or curled my naturally wavy hair, preferring the look of it styled, but tonight I didn't care about any of that.

Not when Mason offered me his hand, pulling me back into the bedroom and tugging me back into bed. He wrapped me in his arms, clearly content to cuddle. I was trying not to freak out. "It's still coming down pretty hard out there. I don't know if you'll be able to get home tonight."

Mason squeezed my hip. "Em?" His voice was calm.

"What?" I whispered, trying to calm my beating heart. I was extra aware of the fact that we were both completely naked, wrapped up in my bed, and I wasn't really sure what any of this meant for *us*.

"*Relax*," he murmured into my ear.

"So… what now?" I yawned. My eyelids felt droopy, like I was fighting to keep them open.

He chuckled. "Now, you sleep." He kissed my bare shoulder.

"Mhmm," I said, shutting my eyes.

Yes, sleep.

Sleep was a good idea.

Maybe in the morning, I'd realize all of this was just a dream.

I woke up hours later with Mason still curled around me. His warmth surrounded me, and I relaxed into his hold. Outside, the storm was still roaring, and I had no idea what time it was.

I couldn't see the snow piling up, but I knew it would. With the skies dumping this much snow, there was no way he'd be able to leave anytime soon. Not until they got the snowplows out here, and power restored. I was just glad we had a generator and had stayed warm throughout the night.

Still, all of this meant that for now… Mason was stuck here. With me.

A smile covered my face as I buried it into his chest.

I couldn't find it within myself to be upset about that.

8

mason

The morning light filtered in through Emily's windows, showing a perfect white winter wonderland outside.

She was still sleeping beside me, and I wondered if I'd ever stop finding her so stunning. She was truly beautiful like this, with her guard down, her lips curled up in the smallest hint of a smile.

Last night had been nothing short of incredible. I wanted to do it again, but I had no idea what Emily wanted from me.

Sitting up, I propped my elbow up on my knee as I looked out the window, lost in thought.

"Looks like it stopped snowing," Emily whispered, distracting me from my thoughts.

I turned back to look at her, finding her lying on her side, the sheet covering those mouth-watering tits I'd had my mouth on last night. "I didn't know you were awake," I told her. "Morning."

"Good morning." She fluttered her eyelashes.

"Looks like it dumped a lot out there last night," I answered, voice rough. "Service is still out. Pretty bad storm."

I'd checked my phone first thing when we'd woken up and wasn't surprised that it wasn't back up.

She yawned, stretching her arms, the sheet slipping down. I tried not to look at her tits, willing my cock not to stand at attention to her delectable body. *Later,* I told myself. If she wanted that. As far as I knew, this was just a one-night thing for her. Just… scratching each other's itches.

But I knew that one night wasn't enough. I wanted her again and again.

"What are we doin' here, Em?"

She furrowed her eyebrows. "We're just having fun, right?"

I swallowed roughly. "Yeah, fun." I dipped my head. "I should probably go check on my truck. See how buried it is." And hopefully, I could grab the duffel bag of extra clothes I kept in the back.

There was an adorable furrow between her brows. "Oh. Right." Was it just me, or did she look… disappointed at the idea I was leaving?

"There's no way I'll be able to go anywhere today," I told her, chuckling. "The roads won't be drivable for a while. Who knows when they'll get the plows out this way?"

She tucked a strand of hair that had come free from her braid behind her ear. "I guess that's true." That seemed to make her relax.

Leaning down, I dropped a soft kiss on her lips. "I keep spare clothes in a bag in my truck just in case. Want to grab them."

Emily nodded. "Okay." She bit her lip. "So…"

"Breakfast?" I asked, interrupting her. She nodded. "You get dressed, and I'll go out to my truck, and then we can figure out something in the kitchen."

"Yeah." Her stomach rumbled as if in answer. "Breakfast sounds good."

"Great." I found my pants, pulling them and my boxers on. The rest of my clothes were upstairs.

I turned to look at her as I leaned against the doorframe, taking her in.

And then, needing the cold air to help clear my head, I headed upstairs to brave the snow.

The snow was deep as I trudged outside, thankful I'd worn a thick coat over here. Luckily, I could get into my truck and get my bag out of it. The Sullivan's house was a ways into the property, but from my brief evaluation, the storm had dumped what felt like almost a foot of snow overnight.

I turned on my truck for a minute, hoping to find an AM radio station where I could listen to the weather, finally finding one. *"A significant winter storm continues this morning across the region,"* they announced. *"Periods of moderate to heavy snow will continue through daybreak. Slick roads, blowing snow, and exceptional cold will make travel dangerous."* The wind whipped around the truck at that moment as if in response, and I shut off my truck, heading inside.

There was no point in staying out here when inside was warm and cozy. I also checked on the generator, topping it off with more propane, hoping we'd have enough to last the length of the storm. We were conserving power wherever possible, but I still didn't want us to freeze if we completely lost it.

Thirty minutes later, Emily joined me in the kitchen, her hair down in loose waves, a light layer of makeup on her face. I'd changed into the clothes from my duffel bag—a pair of gray sweats and a red henley.

"Hey." She smiled at me, leaning her back against the counter next to me.

Emily'd pulled on a pink sweater with black jeans and a pair of cute fuzzy snowman socks that made me grin down at her. "Hi."

"What's for breakfast?" She inhaled deeply. "I didn't expect you to have started without me."

Shrugging, I stirred the eggs in the pan. "I like to cook."

When I'd gone off to college, I found I was grateful for all the time I'd spent with Mom in the kitchen, and I'd been the one who had made dinner for all of my friends once I'd moved off campus. With my ex, I'd made breakfast and dinner for us most nights, too. Until she stopped eating with me altogether. She wasn't hungry in the morning, and she'd work late in the evenings. Maybe that was when everything started to fall apart. We'd drifted apart, and our dreams and goals for the future had changed. *We'd* changed.

"Mason?" When I looked back at Emily, she was frowning. "What's wrong?"

I shook my head. "It's nothing." I didn't want to talk about my divorce. Not right now. "Breakfast is almost done. Do you want coffee? I made some."

Luckily, from growing up spending so much time in the house, I still remembered where everything was. It had made rummaging around the kitchen after getting dressed a lot easier.

"Okay." She gave me a small smile, opening a cabinet and reaching up for a mug. Emily grabbed the milk and a bottle of flavoring, mixing it in until her coffee was lighter than the color of my horse. *Sweet,* I noted. *She likes it sweet.* I wasn't sure why I filed that away for the future, but I did.

It was hard not to notice every little thing about her.

Finishing up our food, I quickly dished everything up onto two plates and carried them over to the island, sliding a plate over to the spot next to me and sitting down.

She surveyed the plate. Eggs, toast, and crispy bacon.

"You didn't have to do all of this," she insisted. "We could have just had, like, cereal or something."

Pointing my fork at her food, I gave her a pointed look. "Eat. You need it after last night."

She made a choking noise, sputtering out her coffee. "*Mason,*" she admonished.

"What?" I gave her a cocky smirk. "I don't know about you, but I worked up quite an appetite."

"You… you're incorrigible." Emily blushed, dipping her face to take a bite of eggs. Her hair fell like a curtain, hiding her face from me.

I brushed it back from her cheek to press a kiss to her skin. "Yep. Better get used to it, darlin'. Especially since you're stuck with me for the next few days. Snow's pretty deep. There's no way we're going anywhere."

She sighed, looking out the window. "I should probably go check on Smokey at some point today."

"Okay. What else do you want to do? Turns out we have a lot of time to kill."

Emily scrunched up her nose. "Well, normally I would just read a book or something. I pre-scheduled all of my content so I wouldn't have to worry about posting and could take a break from all of that, too. So…"

I nodded. "Reading sounds good."

She looked up at me with surprise. "Really?"

"Uh-huh. Your family still has the library, right?" I stroked my jaw in thought, my fingers itching at my beard. I kept it short, and I was definitely going to be overdue for a shave soon.

"Well, obviously. Mom and Dad weren't about to get rid of all their books." Emily gave me a weird look. I remembered when we were younger, all three of the Sullivan kids were always reading. Sure, her older brother Benjamin mostly read comics, but Hunter and I had traded fantasy novels in high school. We'd both loved *The Lord of the Rings*.

When was the last time I sat down and read a book? Years, probably. In Washington, I'd been so busy between work and trying to keep my marriage alive, and ever since I'd moved home, I was trying to keep up with learning how to run the ranch. To take over for dad when he was ready to fully retire and pass the reins down to me.

"Perfect. I remember your dad has a whole bookcase of thrillers. I'll just read one of those."

"Okay." The word was a soft whisper, and when I looked over, Emily had a soft smile on her face, her plate cleaned. It was strange how satisfying I found that.

I reached out, wiping a crumb off her cheek. "Good girl," I said, my voice a low rumble.

She let out a squeak, but I didn't think I missed the heat in her eyes. She *liked it*, I realized. I filed that information away for later, something I definitely planned on pulling out if she wanted a repeat of last night.

Having consumed our food, we cleaned everything up in tandem, enjoying a comfortable silence. A few times, I caught her looking at me, and then dipping her head, cheeks pink. I liked that neither of us needed to say anything, and yet we were shoulder to shoulder, effortlessly acting like…

I shook the thought away. That wasn't what this was, and I knew it. *Fun,* I reminded myself. I could do fun. For now. While I was here, while we were snowed in to this house, I could give her a few orgasms and some fun.

And then at the end, I could walk away.

It wasn't like she was looking for a relationship, anyway. She'd be jet-setting around the world again soon. So there was no point in getting caught up in fantasies of what could have been.

I'd given up my dreams of the future when my ex-wife

had broken my heart. When I'd ended my marriage, the life I'd planned with her since college was suddenly gone, and I'd accepted I might never have it. For a long time, I had been drowning.

Coming back to the ranch had been like drawing my first breath of fresh air in two years. Riding Whiskey through the trails, I'd gotten my head back on right. But as I rode, I still knew I was leaving all of that in the past. My chest ached. It was best not to dwell on it. That was what I kept telling myself. How I kept putting one foot in front of the other. I completely immersed myself in work, figuring that keeping busy would keep my mind off of it, and it had… mostly. Now that I wasn't working, my mind had time to wander. To *think.*

I turned off the sink, and Emily finished drying the last dish.

"Well, *friend,*" I said, trying to ignore how wrong that word felt coming from my lips. I hated it the moment I uttered it, but that was what she wanted, wasn't it? "Time to enjoy our break from reality."

I tended to the fireplace in the living room, and we spent most of our afternoon on either sides of the giant couch. At one point, we headed outside to the barn to check on her horse—but only after I insisted she wear her snow boots *and* her thickest coat. The thriller I'd borrowed from Mr. Sullivan's shelf had only half kept my attention, mostly because I'd spent most of my time staring at Emily, who was engrossed in her romance novel.

She was beautiful. Completely and utterly breathtaking, and I didn't understand how I hadn't noticed before. Though maybe I just hadn't *let* myself. I'd still been a married man, after all.

Now… I was as single as could be. There should have been nothing to stop me from going after what I wanted.

Except something was still holding me back. *She's your best friend's little sister, you jackass,* my brain told me. *That's what's holding you back.* That, and I wasn't sure I deserved another chance at love. I'd thought I'd found my forever the first time, and I'd ended up like this. Who was to say my next relationship wouldn't end just as bad?

Emily yawned, stretching out her arms above her as she closed her book.

I closed mine, too, not caring that I'd lost my place—I didn't remember what was happening, anyway. "You finish?" I asked. She gave me a small nod, setting it on the side table next to her. "How was it?"

Her lips curled up into a tiny smile. "Good. I've been on a paranormal romance kick lately. This one was about a vampire and a witch—" Emily blushed. "God, you probably don't want to know about my book, do you?"

Adjusting my position on the couch and leaning back, I frowned at her. "Why wouldn't I?"

She shook her head. "Most guys, well… They think romance books are a waste of time. That it's silly, and gives women, and I quote, *unreasonable expectations.*" She added air quotes around the phrase.

I blinked, practically seeing red. "They *what?*"

Emily just shrugged. God, I needed to make her understand that whoever had dismissed her in the past—her hobbies, her career, everything—was flat out *wrong.*

"Come here," I murmured, opening my arms wide.

She bit her lip, standing up and sliding in between my open thighs.

"Hi," she whispered as I wrapped an arm around her torso.

"Hi." I kissed her neck. "The things you love aren't a

waste of time, baby." I curled a finger around one of her loose strands of brown hair. "The fact that anyone ever told you it was makes me want to—"

"It's okay," she tried to reassure me, cutting me off. "I'm used to it."

"You *shouldn't* be," I growled. "That's what I'm trying to tell you."

Her eyes met mine, and I saw it all there—the doubt. The fear. God, she was too perfect to have any of this plaguing her. "Thank you," she murmured.

Suddenly, it became my new mission in life to make sure she never heard those words again. That no one ever belittled her ever again.

As long as I lived, I vowed that to myself. Emily Sullivan deserved a life full of happiness and *light.* She deserved to follow her heart wherever it took her.

Even if it took her away from me.

9
emily

I swept my eyes over the spines of the books in our library. My mom might have been all business as a surgeon, but she'd loved reading her whole life. Not just for work, for learning, but for pleasure, and she'd instilled the same love in all her kids. Sure, Benjamin had his nose buried in comic books just as fervently as Hunter read his fantasy novels, but they didn't care what we read, as long as we were reading.

Seeing Mason curled up on the couch with one of my dad's old thriller novels made my heart race. It was so easy having him here. Like this was exactly where he was supposed to be. Like he just *fit*.

Maybe because he'd grown up here, too. Because he'd spent so much time in this house, on our property, it was just natural. But maybe it was something *more*.

He looked up at me, and my heart leapt in my chest. The flutters were hard to ignore. How could I possibly not care about this man? In every action, he showed me how good he was.

"I think you're amazing," Mason told me, holding me

tight against his body. There was something about being held like this that felt comforting in a way I couldn't explain. I was trying really hard not to cry.

No one had ever seemed so angry for me before. Not at me, but for me.

Even though they stung, I was used to it. People only had to make fun of you or make snide comments so often before you believed them.

And yet, Mason's words eased an ache in my heart that I hadn't even realized was there. A sore spot he was already soothing over. I couldn't even see his face unless I strained my neck, given that I was between his legs, but somehow I knew exactly the expression I'd find if I turned around right now.

One I wasn't ready for.

Especially after he'd referred to me as his *friend* earlier. This morning, when he'd asked me what we were doing, I'd freaked out. So I'd told him we were just having fun. Fun, I could do.

There was no way he was ready for the barrage of thoughts inside my mind, anyway. How this felt a little like *fate.* That I'd never woken up next to a man before. I'd never imagined sleeping in someone's arms could feel so right, but they had.

"I think…" I said, turning around in his lap, straddling him. "I think I don't want to talk anymore."

"No?" He raised an eyebrow, sliding his arms around my back and cupping my ass. "Then what do you want to do, darlin'? Start a new book?"

I shook my head, dropping my forehead to his. "No."

He let out a low growl, and then my lips were on his, our bodies wrapped around each other as we kissed, neither of us holding back. Like we knew that our time was limited, and neither of us was going to let a single moment go to waste. Not anymore.

Something about how he praised me, the way he called me *amazing,* the sincerity in his tone, made my insides melt. I was mush in his arms as his tongue stroked over mine, over and over, kissing me with the same precision that he'd had when he fucked me.

God, I loved kissing this man.

It was so unfair.

Unfair because I knew I couldn't keep him. After the storm passed, we'd go back to being virtual strangers. Neighbors, sure, and he'd always be Hunter's childhood best friend, but he'd never be mine.

I ground my hips against him as my hands gripped his red shirt, needy and wanting. Dragging my mouth down his neck, I tugged at his shirt, trying to pull it off his body.

"Emily… *fuck,*" he rasped, both of us pulling apart just long enough for him to help me guide his shirt over his head before he threw it on the ground.

I traced his abs with my fingers. "God, you're fucking *ripped,* cowboy. I wanna trace these with my tongue." It was definitely on my list for the next time we were in bed, lazily exploring each other's bodies. Or maybe in the shower, because I was definitely going to need another one after this.

Rocking my hips again, I felt his hardening cock beneath me. He groaned as I dropped my head to his chest, appreciating his physique and the sexy little happy trail that disappeared beneath his sweatpants.

The sweatpants that were doing *nothing* to hide his current arousal, because I could see the entire outline of his cock.

Suddenly, I could think of nothing I wanted more than tasting him. To make him feel as good as he made me feel. It wasn't just about sex; it was… everything.

Sliding off his lap, I knelt in front of him, tugging on the waistband of his gray sweats.

"What are you doing?" He asked me, frowning.

"Taking care of you," I told him, just like he'd said to me last night.

The fire crackled, and I licked my lips as I pulled his boxers down, freeing his cock. It was magnificent, long and thick, and I wasn't sure how I was going to fit it all in my mouth, but I would try.

His hand slipped behind my head as I reached for his length, wrapping my hand around him and pumping a few times until he's hard as steel, the tip oozing pre-cum and begging for my tongue.

I worked my hand up and down his shaft as I ran my tongue over the crown, flattening it and lapping up his salty taste before running my tongue down his shaft, tracing the veins.

Mason's hands in my hair tightened, and he tilted up my head to force my eyes to meet his.

"Spit on it," he instructed me.

"What?" My eyes widened.

"Spit on my cock, darlin'. Get it all messy for me."

Letting my saliva accumulate in my mouth, I coated his dick in my saliva, doing exactly what he ordered. I let the last few drops drip from my tongue onto his cock. Wrapping my hand around him, I pumped him faster now with the added slickness and took the tip into my mouth, dragging my tongue over the head, paying extra attention to the rim.

"Fuck," he cursed again. "Take your top off, baby. I wanna see those tits while you have your mouth wrapped around my cock."

Baby. That wasn't the first time he'd used the pet name, but I couldn't deny it did something to me.

I moaned around his length, pulling off my sweater,

revealing the black lacy bra I'd put on this morning. I was wearing a matching pair of underwear because… *why not?* They made me feel pretty—sexy. And who didn't want that?

Mason let out a groan as I took him in deeper. "That's it. Choke on my cock like a good girl. Your mouth feels so fucking good, darlin'." His hands pulled at my hair, gathering it up into a ponytail, but he didn't pull me off of his shaft—no. He just used the grip to better leverage my face, helping me as he fucked my mouth.

I squeezed his balls with one hand, the other reaching down and diving underneath my underwear to rub my poor, aching clit. *Yes. This.* This was what I'd needed.

To be used, controlled. Not to have to think anything else, giving him permission over body and soul.

"I'm gonna come," he grunted, tightening his grip on my hair. I sucked harder as Mason slid to the back of my throat, and I almost gagged, having to stop for a moment to breathe in through my nose. "Is that what you want, you little vixen? My cum down your throat?"

I moaned in answer, knowing the vibrations of my throat would only feel better for him. My eyes watered as he fed me another inch of his throbbing cock, the size almost too much for me to handle.

Come just like this, I wanted to encourage him, but I couldn't speak around his shaft. *Down my throat. Let me taste you.* I slipped my pointer finger inside my soaking wet pussy, my body already wound so tight, needing a release.

My body *ached,* and I needed him inside me. To fill me up. To make me see stars the way he had last night. Adding my middle finger, I plunged both inside my entrance, working myself higher. It was only a few moments later, with a sharp growl from Mason, that he spilled inside my mouth, pulling free at the last minute, his cum making a mess out of me, coating my lips and breasts.

Swallowing, I looked up at him from below him, still on my knees, and licked my lips before running a finger through his sticky seed that covered the swells of my chest. "Thank you," I breathed out as I removed my hand from my pants, wiping my fingers on my pajama bottoms.

Mason tugged at my ponytail—not enough to hurt, but enough to distract me from the liquid coating my skin. "Why are you thanking me? I should thank *you*."

I batted my eyelashes. "Because I get the sense that no one's ever done that for you before." And I enjoyed being the one to do it for him. To put him first.

He hadn't opened up to me about his ex-wife yet, but I got the feeling there was more to the story than just the divorce. The way he wouldn't talk about her and would change the subject whenever she was brought up made that all too obvious.

He frowned, tucking himself back into his pants. "No one's ever given me a blowjob?"

I laughed, shaking my head as I ran a hand up his thigh, squeezing it. "Taking care of *you*, Mason. You deserve that too, cowboy." Just like he'd taken care of me last night.

"Oh." He ran his fingers through his hair. "I don't…"

"You don't have to say anything." I looked around, found my top and grabbed it. Before I could put it back on, Mason was off the couch, pulling me into his arms.

"Where do you think you're going?"

"Um." My cheeks flushed, and I used my sweater to cover my bra, knowing my peaked nipples showed through the thin, lacy fabric. "I was thinking we should figure out what we're doing for lunch."

His eyes were molten lava, flaring with heat as he took me in. "Oh, I don't need to think about that." He gave me a wicked grin. "I'm having you, darlin'."

Mason picked me up over his shoulder, giving me the

most delicious view of his ass as he walked. The sweatpants were doing him all kinds of favors.

I don't know what I expected—a bed, maybe?—but he set me down on the dining room table, spreading my thighs and sitting in front of me like I was a goddamn buffet.

And this man liked to *eat.*

"Mason—" I propped myself up on my elbows, ready to protest as he pulled my pajama bottoms off me, then my lacy panties next, but I couldn't come up with a rebuttal as his tongue found my core. He kept licking me, letting out a pleasant hum that went straight to my clit. *"Oh."*

Mason's heated gaze swept over my naked body, and a shiver ran down my body at how intensely he was looking at me. My middle was soft, and I had cellulite on my thighs, and I definitely didn't look the same as I did in my perfectly posed social media photos, but he didn't seem to care about any of that.

I blushed. "You really don't have to—"

"It's your turn," he insisted. His blue eyes pierced me as he looked up at me from between my thighs. "You haven't come yet, did you?"

I shook my head. "No." My voice came out high, all breathy.

He pushed his middle finger inside me, and I let out a whimper. My fingers alone weren't normally enough to get myself there, even if I was wetter than normal. But I couldn't reach that spot inside me, not like Mason could.

"Fuckin' soaked, huh, Em? Did sucking my cock turn you on?" He slipped a second finger inside, pumping into me a few times before pulling them out, his mouth positioning over my core. He blew lightly on my clit, and then I was lost in the pleasure.

"Mmmm," was my only response as he speared my core

with his tongue, thrusting it inside of me over and over. He added his thumb, roughly applying pressure to my clit, and that was all it took. "*Yes,*" I cried out, the orgasm hitting me hard. Wetness coated my thighs, my body hot but satisfied as I dropped my head back, basking in the afterglow of my climax.

"I can't get over how good you taste," he said, pulling back, my release coating his mouth and beard. His eyes were dark, almost black, as he licked me off his lips. "Fucking perfect." He stood up, towering over me on the table, and leaned down to kiss my lips in a lazy exploration of my mouth. Mason stepped into the space between my thighs, grasping my hips until every inch of his body pressed up against me.

Shutting my eyes, I allowed myself to just enjoy his tongue stroking over mine. *Perfect.* He was right. This was perfect. Too perfect, because part of me never wanted it to end. I'd never experienced sex like this before, a lover who was this passionate and giving, and some part of me wondered if I ever would again.

"How is it possible that you're already hard again?" I practically moaned as he pressed his erection against me. I was probably soaking the front of his pants, still sensitive from my orgasm, but he looked completely unfazed.

He bit my lip. "It's because you're so fucking sexy, Emily." God, my name on his lips did things to me. It made me want to take a risk. To stop caring about why it was a bad idea and only think about why it was a good one.

He ran his teeth down my throat. "So. Fucking. *Edible.*"

I fluttered my eyelashes. Reaching out, I slipped my hand between us, palming his length over his sweats. "I want you inside me."

Shoving his pants and boxer briefs down, he ran his hand down his thick length. "You want this cock, huh, needy girl?

Just had it in your mouth and now you need it inside your pretty pussy?"

I nodded, letting out a whine, giving him my best puppy-dog eyes. "Yes, please. I want that. Want you to mess up my insides—"

Mason cut me off with a deep thrust inside of me, sliding all the way to the hilt.

"Oh, God." I groaned. "You feel so good." My fingers gripped the edge of the table as he pulled out slightly before slamming it in again.

Each time he thrust inside, filling me completely, I let out a rough gasp that quickly turned into a low moan.

"Is this what you wanted?"

I nodded, crying out as wave after wave of bliss crashed over me. My eyes drifted shut, head falling back, digging my fingers into the wood, clutching the lip of the table.

He squeezed my thigh, sliding out until only the tip was left inside. "Eyes on me." His hands gripped my hips as he slid in again, slowly this time. Like he was making me *wait*. "I want you to watch me while you come."

Opening them, I found his deep blue eyes focused on me. I reached up for his face, sliding my hands over his dark beard.

He pressed a soft kiss to my lips, and then, with that punishing grip on my thighs, moved in earnest again, fucking me deep.

Outside, the world was a blizzard of white, and in here, it was just the two of us, indulging in each other's bodies. The only sound besides the soft crackling from the fireplace was of skin on skin, each time we came together, and the little gasps and breathy noises I couldn't seem to hold back.

"Ohmygod." I was already hypersensitive from my first orgasm, and it wouldn't take much more for me to come again. It was crazy how well he already seemed to know my body. Like he knew just where to touch me, quickly learning what made me cry out and honing his method.

"That's right," he told me. "Give it to me. Let me hear you. Every gasp, every moan, every whimper. They're all mine." He kissed me roughly, fucking me with his mouth the same way his cock ravaged my insides.

I could feel every punishing thrust inside me, every pump of his hips sliding me back against the table. The only thing that kept me in place was Mason's sturdy hands, that insane grip on my hips. I slid my hands around his neck, clinging to his body, my hard nipples scraping against his chest with every roll of his hips as I tightened my inner muscles around him.

"Fuck, baby," he rasped against my ear, his breath tickling the skin of my throat. "You're going to make me come again." I could feel him throbbing inside of me, how hard he'd gotten, like hot velvet steel.

"Not yet," I moaned, clenching around him again, each tight squeeze making him let out a rough groan that had my nipples hard. "I don't want this to be over yet." It was too good.

"Touch your pretty little clit and make yourself come first," Mason said, giving me a heated look. "I wanna feel that sweet little pussy clenching around my cock as I come." His words were a rasp against my skin, so erotic and dirty, yet painting the most sensual picture of pleasure for me.

I squeezed my pussy at the instruction, reaching down between us until I found my clit. Circling it with my pointer finger, I gathered up my arousal, rubbing it until I let out a soft cry. Spreading my fingers apart into a v shape, I pushed them down until they were on either side of his thick cock, allowing me to feel every vein, every ridge as he moved in and out.

"Feel that?" he said. "Feel the way I'm fucking you?"

Mason switched to short, shallow thrusts that sent sparks down my whole body.

Not even capable of words, just the chanting of his name, over and over and over again.

Mason, Mason, Mason.

I pressed the heel of my hand on my clit, grinding against it as I felt him disappear into my pussy, the way I was stretched out around him with his hard length practically ready to explode. I let out a deep breath, feeling my orgasm coming on but not wanting it to hit yet, trying to savor each snap of his hips. Each pump into me. Even the way his fingers dug into my hips, sure to bruise. I wanted to remember every bit, the bliss he was bringing me.

"Fuuuuuuck," he groaned as I tightened around him one last time, and then neither of us could hold back any longer. He spilled inside of me as I let go, letting out a long moan, my insides fluttering around him. I could feel the way I squeezed his hard, thick cock as he came, spurts of hot cum that filled me up.

"Damn, cowboy," I murmured. "That was one hell of a ride."

He chuckled. "Couldn't have said it better myself, darlin'." Mason gathered me up into his arms, dropping his face to my neck and letting out a deep sigh of satisfaction as he rubbed his hands over my back. I did the same, wrapping my arms around his back as I felt him softening inside of me.

When he finally pulled out, a rush of liquid dripped out of me, streaking down my thighs. His eyes flared as he watched the cum leak, like it was the hottest thing he'd ever seen. "Stay put." Mason's eyes met mine, and then he was on his knees, pressing a kiss to the inside of each thigh.

"What are you doing?" I wasn't sure I was breathing. *Again?* He'd just gone down on me, and then we'd fucked, and he was going to eat me out again? When his cum—and mine—was trickling from my entrance?

"Cleanin' you up." He winked.

"But…" I blushed. "It's *both* of us."

He let out a hum of approval. "Exactly." He licked his lips, and then he swiped his tongue over my slit, licking up every trace before darting inside.

After he'd made me come on his tongue—again—he moved to the kitchen sink to grab a washcloth, turning on the water and waiting for a few seconds until it was warm before getting it damp, and then came back to me. He ran it over my skin, wiping away the sweat and remaining traces of our releases. The warmth felt good, but I was overly sensitive now. Blissfully satisfied, but also feeling slightly raw. He really was huge, and my poor pussy had just taken a pounding.

He helped me down off the table, and I looked around us. Our clothes were strewn everywhere across the living room and kitchen, and I couldn't believe we'd just done that.

My eyes drifted to the outside, where tiny flakes were coming down, the sky darkening once again.

"You know," I whispered, looking out the window. "It's snowing again."

"Good." He gave me a grin that went straight to my core. How was it we had just fucked, and I already wanted him again? This wasn't normal for me.

But then again, I'd never been with a man like Mason before.

"*Good*?" I repeated, raising an eyebrow.

He nodded. "Because, baby, I'm not done with you yet."

And then my stomach rumbled, and we both laughed.

"Food," he said. "Feeding you first it is."

10

mason

After feeding my girl—because she needed it to keep up her stamina—we ended up back on the couch again, with a bunch of candles lit around us.

Unlike earlier, there was no pretense that we weren't spending every second we had left together practically glued to each other. She was tucked against my body, my arms cradling her to my chest, and I'd never felt so peaceful or content.

I'd cooked us steaks over the fireplace, rigging up a grill system since the generator didn't power the entire house. We had the fridge, gas stove, the heater, and the water heater, and that was more than enough.

Was this what my life had been missing before? Was this what I'd been missing for the last few years of my marriage? I'd loved her—at least at one point, I had—but this was different. I couldn't quite put it into words. But there was something about Emily—the way she made me feel so at *home.* So complete.

Like nothing else in the world mattered, as long as I was with her.

I brushed a piece of her hair off her neck and kissed her shoulder. We were dressed again—*unfortunately*—but I already wanted to strip her clothes off and bury my face in her cunt again.

Had I ever been so completely obsessed with someone else's body? There was no stopping my desire for her, my need to bury myself inside of her.

Emily tightened her arms around my back, slowly rubbing her face against my chest.

"Mmmm, darlin'," I hummed, moving my hand back and forth down her back.

"This is nice," she murmured.

Wanting to look at her expression, I pulled back a little. "Couldn't agree more." I tucked a strand of hair back behind her ear. "You know, I meant what I said before."

She blinked at me. "What part?"

"I'm not done with you yet." She'd brushed it off, since we'd both been starving and in desperate need of food, but I wanted her to know that I meant it. "This is…" I shook my head. "There was no way I could have expected this to happen."

Emily let out a small snort. "I know. And this snowstorm might have been unexpected, but I'm glad you're here with me." She interlaced our fingers, running her thumb over my knuckles.

"Me too, Em. Me too." I pressed my lips against her forehead. Needing to touch her. Needing to be close to her. Needing *everything* with her.

I wanted to tell her everything. Why my relationship with my ex-wife had deteriorated. Why I'd moved home. Why I was suddenly dreaming of the future again.

It was too soon. And I knew it. But I couldn't help it.

Her voice was a whisper when she spoke again. "Sometimes I worry, you know… that I've missed out on so much with all the traveling I've done." Emily looked up at the ceiling. "Like, I don't regret it—those experiences were *amazing*, and I enjoyed them so much, but..." She bit her lip. "I never really had time to date. To find someone else to share all of those incredible things with. I guess I'm just... I'm lonely. And I can't help but worry I'll never fall in love or have the life I've always dreamed of."

"Maybe it's not too late," I told her.

She shrugged, tucking her chin against her neck. "I don't know. Maybe it is. Maybe I've wasted all my best years on adventures, and that's it?" Emily asked it like a question, but I wasn't sure it was one.

"You didn't," I reassured her. "You still have plenty of life left to live, Emmie Girl. I promise. You're gonna have that happy ending. Whatever it looks like."

Her glassy eyes caught mine, and there was so much emotion swirling there. "You think?"

"I know it."

And *fuck*, I wanted to tell her I knew it because I wanted to give her that. That she didn't need to find the right person for her, because I was here.

I didn't want to give her up at the end of this, even though it was crazy and we'd barely spent any time together since she'd been back. But I *knew* her. I didn't need a month or more to realize what I knew that first night at the bar.

She was too good for me. Too young. And she deserved the world.

Could I give her that? *Yes.*

But I didn't know what she wanted.

If when she closed her eyes at night, she saw the same thing as me. Little brunette children on horseback. Braids whipping in the wind as they ran through the field. Tiny overalls and cowboy boots. A house full of laughter, of kids, of love. A pregnant wife, waiting for me, dressed in a green gingham dress that curled over her belly and matched her emerald eyes, her brown hair loose and wavy at her back.

My heart ached. The dream was so vivid, so real. Like I could almost reach out and touch it.

Because I wanted it. So damn bad. And it was *right there* in my grasp. Then it was gone, and I was back in front of the fire, holding her in my arms.

"Mason?" she asked, then let out a giant yawn.

I lifted her up in my arms. "Come on, darlin'. Time for bed. We had quite a day, didn't we?"

Emily gave me a small roll of her eyes as I walked towards the stairs. "We didn't do anything. What are you talking about?"

My answering grin was wicked. "Didn't do *anything*, huh?" I smacked her ass. "Brat."

She did her best to look innocent as I dropped her onto the bed. "Uh-uh."

"So you're not sore?" I slid my hand up her thigh, slipping my hand underneath her waistband and sliding two fingers inside of her.

She let out a rough moan as I moved them inside of her—doing my best not to be too rough—then she gave me a small whimper. "*Mason.*"

Pressing soft kisses on her lips, I pulled my fingers out. "I know, baby, I know." Pulling her sweater off, followed by her pajama pants, I took my time, memorizing her body with the sweep of my lips, giving her tender touches and gentle caresses.

She fell asleep before I made it back up to her lips, her breath evening out into a steady breath. I quickly shed the rest of my clothes, stripping down to just my boxer briefs, and then I slid both of us under the covers.

And then I pulled her into my arms and promptly fell asleep.

When I woke up, Em was pressed up against me, one leg thrown over mine, her face nuzzled into my bare chest. It felt so fucking right, waking up with her like this. Like this was what I'd been missing for the last year. Like somehow, Emily Sullivan was the missing piece I'd needed in my life.

Was it crazy? Yes.

But I couldn't deny it. I wasn't sure I wanted to anymore. Something about her was deep in my veins, lighting me up inside.

Another day, another week, another month—I'd take whatever time I had left with this woman. With this vixen that filled me with a burning passion I'd never felt before.

My aching cock pressed against her belly, and she let out a little sigh in her sleep.

The morning light filtered in the window, practically illuminating her in gold. She was beautiful.

"Emily," I murmured in her ear, brushing her hair over her neck so I could press soft kisses to her skin.

"*Mmm*," she answered with a sleepy smile on her face, like she was still dreaming. I wondered what she was dreaming about.

Me? I hoped she was dreaming about me. Fuck, but I wanted her to be dreaming about me.

Trailing my fingers down her body, I swept my thumbs over her nipples, enjoying the little whine she gave from my touch. Then lower, till I reached the seam of her panties, pressing my thumb over her core. A damp spot was already forming, and fuck. Was she turned on right now?

The fact that her hot, wet pussy was covered right now was a travesty. I hooked my fingers into the waistband, dragging them off her body until she was bare for me.

"Wake up, Em," I said, dragging my lips over the sensitive

skin of her neck. "Wake up so I can fuck you properly. Like I've been aching to do since last night."

Truthfully, I burned for her. She needed to stay warm? I'd keep her warm. Forever. No questions asked.

She let out another moan, but didn't stir further as I slipped a finger inside, feeling her cunt squeeze around me.

"Fuck me," I groaned. "You're the most beautiful thing I've ever seen." I added another finger, pumping her slowly. Like I'd started to last night, but it had been obvious that she was sore. But God, that didn't keep me from wanting her.

Her eyes fluttered as I worked her higher, more and more breathy noises slipping from her lips. She moaned as I scissored my fingers inside of her, her back arching off the bed. *"Mason."*

She hadn't opened her eyes yet, but I knew she was awake.

"Tell me you want this," I said against her ear as I pulled my fingers free from her core. "Tell me you want me buried deep inside of you."

"Yes," she cried, her eyes fluttering open as she slid her hands up my bare chest. "Please, Mason." She opened her legs wider, the one thrown over my body pushing higher, and I couldn't hold back anymore.

Pushing my boxers down, I fisted my cock, giving it a few rough tugs.

"You're not too sore, are you?" I asked her. Guiding the tip to her entrance, I rubbed it through her arousal, covering it in her wetness.

She shook her head. "No. Fuck me. Don't make me beg."

Emily let out a little whine as I thrust inside of her, slow and deep. She was so wet, her insides welcomed me with no hesitation. "Darlin'," I said against her skin, pressing a kiss to each of her hardened nipples as I rolled my hips, sliding in deeper with every movement. "You never have to beg for anything from me."

This was more intimate, less frenzied and desperate. We kissed lazily as I pumped inside of her, like we were in no rush to get to our destination, just enjoying the journey.

Emily's hands wound around my neck, her perfectly manicured fingernails digging into my shoulder blades as she gasped into my mouth, and I slid my hands up and down her spine.

Fuck, I wanted to start every morning like this. That I could wake her up like this every single day. There had never been anywhere I wanted to be more than right here, buried between Emily Sullivan's thighs.

"You're so fucking perfect," I murmured against her mouth.

She tightened her grip on me, curling her leg tighter around me, pulling me in deeper to her body.

But there was no urgency or rush, just the two of us losing ourselves in each other's bodies. I didn't want this moment to end, didn't want to wake up from this dream. Because it was a dream.

Spending time with her like this felt like *more*. Like the vision I'd had last night could almost come true.

I want you, I wanted to say. *I need you.*

We came together, our bodies intertwined, with my lips saying what I couldn't in words.

Pulling her onto my chest, I kept my cock buried inside of her, letting her rest her head on my chest. She ran her fingers through my chest hair, humming softly as I played with her hair.

Outside, it looked like the storm had slowed down. The sky was a beautiful bright blue, the sun shining, and I hoped that would be a good sign. It would be worse if it melted off and then froze again, but I had to hope that wouldn't happen.

Because if it did, the ice would cause more problems than the deep snow.

"Looks like the worst of the storm has passed," I told her softly as she stretched out her arms. "I need to see if I can listen to the radio for some updates, but we definitely won't be able to go anywhere until they get the snowplows out."

It would probably take another few days. In the city, they'd be more apt to plow right away, but out in the country? We'd be lucky if we got unburied within a few days.

Not that I cared.

I'd be happy staying right here—buried between her thighs—for the rest of my life.

11
emily

There was something extra peaceful about the world out my window this morning. It was calm and beautiful, even with the world buried under a blanket of white. Though maybe that had nothing to do with the snow, and everything to do with the man at my side. Mason had woken me up with his fingers before fucking me slow and deep, and I honestly couldn't remember a better way to wake up.

Knowing the storm would pass soon, that we'd have to go back to reality, had me feeling slightly apprehensive. I had no idea what would happen to us once the snow cleared. It was like we were in a perfect little bubble, and neither one of us wanted to pop it by bringing up the dreaded question.

"We should probably get up," I murmured, looking outside at the snow. "Maybe we can divert some of the propane to the hot tub." My parents had gotten it a few years back, and I loved it.

He wiggled his eyebrows. "Oh, the hot tub, huh?" He slid his fingers through my entrance, making me let out a sharp whimper. "And you're not sore?"

I winced. "Maybe, a little." He was just so big, and my body still wasn't used to the stretch yet—even if we'd spent most of the last two days having sex. When he'd pulled out, I'd felt the loss instantly.

Mason laughed, kissing me softly. "I'm sorry, baby."

Kissing him back, I hummed. "Worth it."

He grinned, running his fingers through his dark brown hair, flashing me a look that promised a repeat later.

God, if only my childhood self could see me now.

"You know, eight-year-old me was obsessed with you." I rested my head on his bare chest, looking up at his handsome face. I used to follow my brother and him around everywhere, so in love with my older brother's best friend, in the purest way possible. He'd always been so kind to me, even when he had no reason to be. Mason could have brushed me off—I was just a kid, and he wasn't obligated to do anything for his best friend's little sister—but he hadn't. Maybe that was why I'd loved him.

Maybe that was why I still did.

"Yeah?" Mason ran his fingers through my hair, a little smirk forming on his face. "And what about twenty-eight-year-old you?"

I hummed. I was *definitely* still obsessed with him. "Maybe." Looking up at him through my eyelashes, I couldn't help but notice the way he was looking at me.

Like I was something sacred. It made my smile fall. Because part of me knew that this wasn't just *fun*. Maybe it had started out like that, but it didn't feel like just fun or just a meaningless hookup, not anymore. But I was the one who told him we were just having fun, like an idiot.

This morning felt like… I looked up at him, at his handsome face. That scruffy beard and mustache that I loved feeling between my thighs, on my skin. Those blue eyes that were always trailing over my body, like he was trying to commit it to memory.

This morning felt a lot like making love. And I didn't know what to do with that. I'd never been in a serious relationship, not really. I'd had flings, but they had never felt as monumental as we did.

Which was crazy, wasn't it? I was almost twenty-nine, and I'd never been in love. When I'd confessed that last night, it felt like the world was going to open up and swallow me whole.

I was *terrified* that I would never fall in love. Never meet the right man, get married—start a family.

Because I wanted that *desperately*. Even more after seeing my brothers welcoming their children into the world, how happy they'd been cradling those babies in their arms.

And here was Mason. Mason, who'd been married before. He didn't seem to want to talk about it or his divorce. That was okay—even if I desperately wanted to understand. Because I wanted to know him better than I knew anyone else.

If I were being truthful to myself, maybe I'd admit that it never felt like just a fling. It always felt like more.

Because this was Mason. My Mason.

"Well, that's good." He interlaced our fingers before bringing our hands up to his mouth and kissing the back of mine. "Because I'm a little obsessed with you, too, darlin'."

Giggling, I poked at his stomach. At those rock-hard abs I'd had my tongue on earlier. That I wanted to admire all over again. "Mason. Have you seen yourself? I had a crush on you from the moment I realized boys weren't, in fact, *gross*," I admitted. "But back then, I was just your best friend's annoying little sister, and that's okay."

"I never thought you were annoying," he grumbled.

Smiling, I laid my head in the crook of his arm, closing my

eyes as he played with my hair. "I was, though. Constantly coming up with excuses to be near you. Asking you to teach me how to ride a horse. Getting hurt and then asking you to put my bandaids on." I looked down at our hands. He'd been rubbing his thumb over my skin, over and over. "Even though my parents were doctors."

With that, Mason smiled. "I thought it was cute, you know. You with those little pigtails and your pink cowgirl boots. But you never complained about it being hard or gave up. It's one of the things I like about you, Em. Even now, you're so dedicated. And you're just…" He shook his head. "You're mesmerizing, you know that?"

"I don't know about that…" I mumbled the words, trying to hide my blush.

"I do." He nodded to himself. "I see it, even now. With the way you've worked so hard these last few years, tryin' to prove to all the naysayers that you can be successful doin' what you love. Making a name for yourself, not because of your parents but because of *you*."

My eyes filled with tears. Mason reached up, brushing them away.

"I wish you could see yourself the way I do," Mason murmured against my skin.

"You barely even know me," I told him. "We're hardly any more than strangers."

"That's not true, and you know it. I know you, Emily." He pressed his lips to my neck, and I resisted letting out a small moan.

"I was *ten* when you left for college," I reminded him.

He scoffed. "I saw you after that. Don't act like I was never around after graduating high school."

"Can you blame me? You left, and then you came back with a girlfriend. Broke my little heart, even though I knew you'd never be mine. Not really. Still, I'd always thought that somehow, once I grew up, you'd see *me*."

"I see you now, Emily Sullivan," he whispered against my neck. "I see all of you, and damn, baby. I never want to look away. I hate I didn't notice you sooner," he murmured.

"Why would you have?" I shook my head. I'd been so much younger, and then… he'd been married.

"You know what I mean, Em. Two years ago, I…" He swallowed, looking down and not meeting my eyes. "The marriage wasn't great. And in my heart, I'd already moved on. But God, seein' you at Hunter's wedding *undid* me. You in that pale green dress, the way you were practically glowing with happiness as you danced on the beach? *Fuck.*" The rasp of his voice against my ear made me shudder. Mason pressed his lips to my shoulder. "So beautiful. Better than any Montana snowstorm, baby." There was something about those words from his lips, about the reverent way he looked down at me, that made the sincerity in his words so apparent. "I was an idiot. I wasted so much time. If I'd have known… fuck."

Sometimes, it felt like this was inevitable. That this week was the universe putting up every sign, screaming, *Here he is, the man of your dreams.* But it had been so long since I'd really trusted someone else enough to feel safe. To feel vulnerable. It had been so long since I'd trusted *myself.* Like I was worried that if I opened up my heart, if I gave it away, it would be broken. And one more crack felt like enough to break me.

But maybe with Mason, I could feel safe enough to fall. Maybe I could drown in him, could keep falling endlessly into those pools of baby blue, and never worry about resurfacing. Somehow, I knew he'd keep me afloat.

"Mason…" I murmured, aware of the fact that I'd just been staring at him for several minutes. What was there to say? It was so soon. It was too soon. But also, it felt *right.*

Being here, wrapped up in his arms, snuggled in my bed to keep warm with the power out, felt right.

And that honestly scared the hell out of me.

"I know, Em," he said, brushing his lips over my skin. "I know."

"Will you tell me about her?" I whispered. "Your ex? What happened between you two?"

He shut his eyes. "I don't want to dwell on the past. Not when I'm here with you."

I smiled, cupping his cheek. "I just want to understand, cowboy."

Letting out a sigh, he pulled me in tight, then sat up, leaning against my headboard and keeping me in his lap. Like he couldn't deny me anything.

"My ex-wife…" Mason started, his thumb brushing against the nape of my neck over and over, in a motion that was distracting me more than I cared to admit. "She wasn't a bad person, you know? I don't resent her for her decisions."

I didn't know, not really. Still, I nodded, because what else could I say?

"It was great for a long time. We met freshman year, and we hit it off right away. Then we started datin', and by the time we graduated, well… the next logical step was getting engaged. We'd already lived together for a year by then, anyway. So I bought a ring." He swallowed roughly. Somehow, I understood he needed to get this off his chest. That he needed to say this. So I stayed silent. "Don't get me wrong. I always wanted to get married." He chuckled. "I loved the idea of being a husband. And maybe I loved it more than I loved her." He winced. "Things didn't get bad for a while. We'd always talked loosely about havin' kids, ever since we were young, and I thought that's what we were workin' towards. But she always insisted it wasn't the right time. She had to work too much. Or she'd just gotten a promotion. Or we needed a bigger house. But over time, I realized those were all excuses."

"Mason…" My heart broke for him.

"And maybe we were never right for each other, not really. Maybe we just wanted different things. We'd just spent so long together that I'd gotten used to it. Still, I tried my hardest to make it work. Our daily rituals became distant memories until I was spendin' most of my time alone and wonderin' how I'd gotten there. Nothing was what I'd hoped for. I'd left the ranch behind 'cause she wanted to live in the city. I was wearing a suit every day, and nothing I was doing felt like *me.* And then, my wife didn't even want to spend time with me. Suddenly I didn't know who I was anymore. But that wasn't even the deal-breaker. I…" His voice was unsteady when he spoke again. I spun in his lap, placing my hand over his heart. Like I could sense that he needed the support. "I wanted a family." Mason shook his head, his eyes haunted. Like he was *hurting.* "I kept asking, pushing for it. My ex-wife… she'd always known that. I'd never hidden that I wanted kids. Things weren't good, but I thought maybe we could still work through it. We'd been fightin' so much, but…" He choked up. "The night of Hunter's wedding was the end for me. One of Gabbi's bridesmaids had a six-month-old."

I nodded, a smile touching my face. "Abigail." One of her best friends—Charlotte—and her husband had a baby a year ago. She'd been adorable, wearing a fluffy little yellow dress, sitting on Daniel's lap during the ceremony.

"Adorable kid," Mason said. "I brought it up to her, then, seeing how happy the three of them looked. A sweet little family. Told her that maybe it was time, and we should have one of our own. We weren't getting any younger, after all. We'd been married for a decade. But suddenly, I didn't recognize her at all. She said she didn't want a family, Em." He looked down at his lap, sliding his hands down till they rested on my hips. "That she didn't want kids at all. She'd changed her mind. I was devastated. The woman I'd married was gone, and in her place was a stranger."

"She never told you before?" My question was hardly more than a whisper.

"No. But maybe…" he sucked in a breath. "Maybe I just wasn't enough." His eyes were glassy, and fuck, my heart broke for him.

"You're enough, Mason. Of course you are."

"I don't blame her for changing her mind. I just can't help but feel like I wasted so much time, you know? That was what hurt the most. She never told me she didn't want to start a family together until the end." Mason looked down at his lap. "Turns out she was spending a lot of time at work with one of her coworkers with all her long hours in the office. I didn't think anything of it. Of course I didn't. And now…

"And now they're getting married, next year," he finished, leaning his head back against the headboard. "We parted on good terms. I don't hate her, Emily. Of course I don't. It's just…"

"She should never have let you go," I whispered, running my fingers through his hair. "I know I wouldn't have."

He shut his eyes, tears trailing down his cheeks, and I kissed them off, taking my time as he clung to my body, holding me tight.

I sensed he needed this hug more than anything. Had he ever mourned the end of his marriage? Had he ever *cried?* I got the sense that he hadn't. That he'd been bottling it up inside of him all this time.

"I'm sorry," I told him. "You deserve everything, Mason. The life you dream of."

His damp blue eyes met mine, and he kissed me softly.

I couldn't read the emotion on his face. I wasn't sure I was ready to.

He slid back inside me, making me gasp as his cock filled me, burying to the hilt, and once more, we lost ourselves in each other's bodies, clinging to each other with everything we had.

Mason closed his eyes, sinking into the warm water.

It had taken us a lot longer to leave my bed than I'd planned, but we got the hot tub on and as soon as it was hot, we'd sunk inside, the water seeming to melt away all our problems.

Thankfully, my parents' property was extensive enough that I didn't have to worry about someone seeing us, or any sort of propriety. We'd wrapped ourselves up in fluffy white bathrobes for the walk outside, but neither of us had bothered to find a swimsuit before slipping into the water.

I let out a happy moan as it soothed my muscles, my body relaxing almost immediately.

We didn't talk about what had just happened. About everything he'd told me, or how I'd held him as he cried, or how we'd made love again as he held me to his body.

Maybe we didn't need to. Maybe some things were better left unsaid.

The world was still. Pine trees were dusted with snow, everything covered in a thick coat of white, like even the universe needed to take a breath.

Maybe we needed this too.

Maybe we needed each other.

I climbed onto his lap, winding my fingers into his hair. "Hi," I murmured, scratching my fingernails through his scalp.

He let out a moan, eyes fluttering shut. "That feels so fucking good, Em."

"Good." My words were barely a whisper. "Are you feeling better?"

His blue eyes blinked open, holding mine. "Yes. Thank you. I'm sorr—"

"You don't have to apologize," I told Mason, cutting him off. "Not for having feelings. And definitely not for the way she broke your heart." I placed my hand on his chest, over his heart, feeling it pounding under my touch. "Okay?"

He nodded. "Okay." He looked like he'd just had a realization—like something important had flickered through his face, even for only a moment.

Scooting further onto his lap, I let my hardened nipples press against his chest. "Okay," I repeated.

Mason brought his hands up to my thighs, rubbing up and down as I rested my forehead against his, just soaking up his presence. Neither of us moved for a long time, except for our hands as they rubbed and soothed. Like somehow, this was healing every wound, every broken piece inside of us.

As if we were getting ready for something entirely new to begin.

12
mason

I hadn't expected to confess everything about my ex to Emily, but it felt cathartic, somehow. Like I'd needed to get it off my chest—needed to let it go—so I could move on. So I could look forward to a new future.

Hopefully, one where the beautiful woman in front of me stayed by my side.

Was it too much to ask?

She'd kissed the tears off my face, for fuck's sake. No one had ever done that for me before.

And now, with her nipples pressed against my chest, her soft, wet body straddling mine, I couldn't find myself to be upset about the circumstances that had happened. Because they'd led me here—to her.

"Emily," I murmured, slipping my hand around the back of her neck. "What are you doing to me?" She shook her head as I kissed her bare skin on her throat, sucking it into my mouth. "God, I don't deserve you." I gripped her thighs tighter, pulling her until there wasn't an inch of our bodies that weren't touching.

"You do," she said, cupping my cheek and rubbing her thumb over my beard. "You do, Mason."

Her eyes were shining as I pulled back, looking into her eyes.

She moved back, as if she were going to get off of me, but I shook my head, keeping hold of her body. "Come on. Let me hold you."

A nod, and then she relaxed against my chest, both of us letting out a sigh as we let the heat of the hot tub warm us from the inside out. I didn't know how badly I'd needed this.

Someone to hold. I'd missed having someone to talk to, someone to share my feelings with. Someone who I could be myself with.

"I didn't freak you out earlier, did I?" I brushed a piece of damp brunette hair behind her ear. "With all of that?" It was a lot to confess at once, I knew.

She shook her head, her fingers tracing circles on my abs under the water. "No. Honestly, it was a relief."

"A relief?" I frowned. "How so?"

Emily looked up at me with a sheepish expression on her face. "I just couldn't help but wonder, you know. What went wrong? If you were still in love with her. But…"

"But I'm not."

"Yeah. I guess I just would have felt guilty, you know? If you had unresolved feelings."

"I don't. Not anymore. I'm glad that's all in the past. It hurt, but now I'm here." I gestured around us. "Back in Montana. Back on the ranch. And…" I rubbed a thumb over her cheekbone. "Here with you."

She sucked in a breath. "Yeah. Me too."

"Good."

I kissed her softly, but it quickly turned to more. Fuck, how could I already want her again? Her fingers found my length under the water, wrapping around my cock, and she pumped me slowly.

"We can't seem to keep our hands off each other," I said with a groan.

Emily gave me a sexy little smirk. "And why would we want to, cowboy? I told you, I'm *obsessed* with this body."

"That's not what you said," I grunted as she ran her thumb around the head. "You said you were obsessed with *me*, baby."

She dropped her lips into a little pout that had me wanting to fuck her mouth again. "There's a difference?" She batted her eyelashes, squeezing her tits between her arms.

I gripped the back of her neck, forcing her mouth to mine. "Of fucking course there is, darlin'. I'm obsessed with *you*. I can't get enough of you. Your body is just… *fuck*. It's like whipped cream on top of hot chocolate. You might not need it, but, fuck, if it doesn't taste like heaven."

Emily giggled as I bent my head down, capturing one of her nipples with my teeth, sucking it into my mouth. Her giggle quickly turned into a low moan as I licked and sucked, nipping the tiny bud before switching sides and giving the other one the same attention. Keeping her stuck in place with my tight grip on her thighs, she kept pumping my shaft as I worshipped her breasts and those pretty pink nipples. "I want to fuck these," I told her, before tugging on her nipple with my teeth. "Want to feel your tongue on my cock as I thrust between 'em."

She let out a whimper as her head dropped back, hair falling into the tub.

"Is that a yes?" I asked, looking up at her with a wicked expression on my face.

My girl just nodded. "Whatever you want, Mason," she gasped.

I spread her thighs apart, opening her legs for me, and slid two fingers inside of her. She was still wet from earlier, especially with my cum still leaking out of her.

It was a dangerous game we were playing, even if she was on birth control. But some *part* of me secretly loved the idea of knocking her up—of watching her belly grow round with our baby. A little cowgirl just like her momma, who would run around our ranch in pink boots with a bow in her hair.

"I want you," she told me. "However and whenever you want."

"Whenever?" Fisting her hair, I tugged lightly on it. "Don't say that to me, Em, or you're never going to be wearing panties again. I'll have you sitting on my cock twenty-four seven. You can keep it warm for me, baby." My cock twitched at the thought. Of having her whenever I wanted.

She moaned, clenching around my fingers.

"You like that, huh? You wanna be my good girl, ready to be fucked whenever I want?"

"*Yes,*" she cried, an orgasm hitting her as she came on my fingers.

God, she was beautiful when she came like this, her expression melting into one of pure pleasure, her eyes a little hazy, a tiny smile on her lips.

"Fuck." I pulled my fingers out of her body, wrapping my hand over hers where she still had a grip around my length. "There might be some resistance—"

I'd never fucked anyone in a hot tub before, but the water posed a few challenges.

But she just shook her head, lifting her hips and together, we guided my tip to her entrance. She sank down onto my length, just a few inches, before letting out a rough cry. Goddamn, but she felt hotter than normal inside, and even tighter than usual.

"Baby," I moaned. "Oh, *fuuuck.*" She lifted her hips before plunging back down again, like she was desperate to impale herself on my cock.

She did it a few more times, working herself down to the base, but the friction from the water was quickly becoming too much. I grabbed her hips, lifting her out of the water while keeping myself buried inside of her. Setting her down on the side of the tub, she wrapped her arms and legs around me as I started to piston in and out of her, fucking her deep.

"Is this what you needed, huh? A good, hard fuck?"

Emily cried out, dropping her head back as I slammed in to the hilt, making her tits bounce. The sunlight bounced off the snow and illuminated her skin, making her look almost ethereal.

"Yes, yes, yes," she chanted. "Mason."

God, my name on her lips was incredible. The way her sweet voice sounded, her green eyes baring into mine as I fucked her in earnest—it was too much. I wanted to make this last, wanted to draw out her orgasm—to edge her until she was crying out, panting and shaking—but I would never make it. Not when her tight cunt felt like heaven, and I was already extra sensitive from fucking her earlier this morning.

"You're a dream," I rasped in her ear. "A fucking beautiful dream. One I never want to wake up from."

I didn't know if she'd heard me—if she was even cognizant at the moment—but I didn't care. Let her have my confession. If she looked at it too quickly, she'd realize how I felt. How far I'd come from our original agreement.

This was so much more than just a casual fling, than just sex. This was a raw connection that I couldn't deny, even if I wanted to.

And I didn't.

I just wanted her.

❄

When I woke up the next morning, I could somehow feel a shift in the air. Like something was different now. Somehow, the world had changed overnight—and so had we. It was sobering, really. My phone buzzed, and a part of me knew what it meant.

Our little bubble of paradise was over.

The bed next to me was empty, and I rolled over, finding her standing in the doorway. The lights illuminated her body, bathing her in a warm light. Like the angel she was.

"Power's back on," she told me. "I haven't gone outside to turn the generator off yet, but..."

"I can do it. Just let me get dressed. Looks like they got the cell towers back up again."

"Yeah." Emily bit her lip as she leaned against the doorframe, wearing only my shirt. God, I would never get used to that sight. "I got ahold of my parents this morning. They were worried about me, but they're having a great time on their trip. I told them I was fine."

She climbed onto the bed, straddling my lap. I wound my hands around her, cupping her bare ass and squeezing lightly. Emily wasn't wearing any panties—damn vixen that she was. Like she'd taken my suggestion yesterday to heart.

"And are you fine?" I asked her, kissing her neck.

She shook her head. "Not really."

I knew what she meant. "I have to go home," I told her, even though I had no desire to leave her. "I need to check on things at the ranch, and Whiskey..."

She gave me a sad smile. "I know." Emily ran her fingers through my hair. "We always knew this would have an expiration date, didn't we?"

I shook my head, gripping her backside. "It doesn't have to. Come with me."

"What do you mean?" She looked confused.

"Come back with me, back to my cabin. I don't want this to end."

Her eyes widened. "I…"

I kissed her passionately, needing her to understand what I was saying. "Come with me, not because you have to because of the storm. Not because we're stuck together, but because you want to. Say yes for no other reason than you want to be with me."

She worked her lower lip between her teeth, as if she was trying to work it out inside her head. "But, Mason…"

I knew what she was going to say. That we'd never work. But that wasn't true, and we both knew it now.

"I want to see where this thing is going. You can see it too, can't you? That we could be so good together. Maybe it's crazy, but I like to think it was fate. Walking into that bar that night—finding you there—and then these last few days together. It felt *right*."

Emily's hand rested on my cheek, rubbing slightly at the scruff there. "How long are we talking?"

"Through Christmas, if I can convince you. But I'm not going anywhere, baby. This—you—are all I want. All you have to do is say yes."

She shut her eyes, her breath coming out rough. And then she smiled. "Okay."

"Yeah?"

"Yes."

And then I kissed her—because I was fucking ecstatic. It might not have been forever—but it was a start.

This is where you live?" Emily's eyes widened as she took in the cabin. It had taken us a few hours to tidy the house, plus turning off the generator and making sure everything was still in working condition after the storm.

I'd called my mom as Em packed her bags, and she'd reassured me that my dad was getting the road between our properties plowed as we spoke.

It felt strange coming back here. Like I was a different man now than I was when I'd left it days ago. And looking over at the woman in the front seat, the one whose thigh my hand rested on, maybe I was.

I ran my free hand through my hair, trying to see this place through her eyes. Her parents lived in a giant house. Would she think it was too small, too shabby? "Yeah," I said, looking at the A-frame building.

"Mason, it's beautiful." She placed her hand over her heart. Her green eyes practically sparkled when she looked back at me.

My heart leapt, unprepared for the unbidden reaction to her soft smile. "Really?"

"Uh-huh." She nodded, leaning in to kiss me quickly. "Will you show me around?"

I grinned. "Gladly." Getting out of the truck, I walked around to her side, opening her door for her. I slid my hands around her waist, lifting her out onto the truck and setting her down in the soft, powdery snow. She interlaced our fingers, and we walked together towards my cabin. I'd go back for our bags later.

Sweeping her up into my arms, I took the steps up to the deck two at a time, and didn't put her down until I'd unlocked the door and carried her inside.

Something about this moment felt monumental.

Like carrying my bride in over the threshold.

She wasn't—but damn if I didn't want her to be. *Too soon, Mason,* I tried to remind myself. I was getting ahead of myself, and I needed to slow down.

But secretly, I couldn't help but hope.

13
emily

It took me a moment to remember where I was. Yesterday, I'd gone home with Mason.

We'd even gone back for Smokey, taking a small horse trailer and bringing her back with us. It felt right, seeing my mare stabled up next to Mason's strong, brown stallion. My heart had fluttered at the sight. At some point, we'd take them for a ride together. I already had goosebumps, thinking about riding side by side on the trail with Mason. We hadn't done that since we were kids.

Reaching over, I yawned, but the spot beside me was empty—the man himself no longer in bed with me.

His cabin was so cozy and warm, and I could see little touches of him everywhere I looked. Secretly, I loved it. I loved being in his space, that smelled like him—juniper berries and pine and musk. It felt like I was surrounded by everything he loved, surrounded by *him*. I loved it.

Probably because I was falling in love with him.

In every little action, every little way he showed he cared about me.

I could smell the scent of coffee and eggs in the air as I

rolled out of his bed, found his discarded forest green henley from the night before and pulled it on over my head.

There was no point in trying to find my panties—God knows he'd just take them off of me again, anyway.

I'd never had this much sex in my entire *life*. There had to be some limit, didn't there? Mason's stamina was insane. Maybe it was because of all the manual labor he did out on the ranch. God, there was something about cowboys. Though maybe it was just this cowboy.

My cowboy. That thought brought a smile to my face as I found him in the kitchen, wrapping my arms around his waist as he stood in front of the stove. He'd put on a tight t-shirt and boxers, leaving those delicious veiny forearms bare for me to admire.

"Good morning," I mumbled against his muscular back.

"Mornin', darlin'," he said, letting out a deep chuckle. "Didn't know you'd woken up. I was gonna bring you breakfast in bed."

"Oh." I unwound myself from him. That was sweet. "Well, I woke up, and the bed was empty, so I came looking for you."

He leaned over, kissing my forehead. "It'll be done in a moment. There's a mug of coffee for you on the counter." He tilted his head, and I followed the motion, finding a mug waiting for me.

"So… what do you want to do today?" I asked him, leaning against the counter next to the stove.

Mason grinned. "I was thinking we'd go into town since the roads are all pretty much clear."

"Into town?" I repeated, raising an eyebrow. "Why?"

"Come on, baby. You don't want to go back to Giddy Up and have a do-over of our first night?"

"Hmmm." I pretended to think about that. And while that sounded fun—especially because we hadn't gotten to dance together that night—I thought spending the day here in his cabin sounded even better. "No." I stuck my tongue out at him.

He laughed as he plated up the food. "Nah. Was thinking we'd go to the tree lot and get a tree. Jonah owes me a tree."

"A tree?" I looked around his cozy cabin. "But you already have one?" I pointed to the corner. It was a smaller tree, nothing like the giant ones my mother used to get, but it was beautiful, decked out in ornaments. I wondered if his mom had decorated it for him. Though knowing him, he'd probably done it himself. "Sure. But *you* don't have a tree. So let's go get you one."

My mouth dropped. "Really?"

He turned to face me. "Why not? It'll make you happy."

I didn't even bother with words. Just wrapped my arms around his stomach, burying my face in his chest and giving him the biggest hug I could muster. "Thank you," I whispered.

"Don't have to thank me, darlin'." His finger brushed under my chin, tilting my head until my eyes met his. "Now, let's eat, and then we'll go find you a tree."

We were walking through the Cassidy's tree lot, fingers interlaced, a steaming hot cup of hot chocolate—with whipped cream—in both of our hands. Honestly, this felt like a dream.

And I knew everyone was looking at us. Most people knew who we were—me, because of my parents being surgeons, and Mason, because of his family's ranch. I looked up at him, wondering if we looked right together. He was a lot taller than me, and yes, he was older, but the eight year difference didn't bother me. Not at this point in my life.

Besides, we wanted the same things. Knowing that had made a lot of my fears melt away. Mason asking me to come home with him, to *be with him*, that had made the rest.

I didn't know exactly what we were—we hadn't labeled it, but I was happy. Waking up next to him, the way he rested his hand on my thigh as he drove, even the way he held my hand. All of it was new, and yet, we'd slipped into it as easily as breathing. Honestly, this felt like our first official date, and the thought had me giddy.

"What about that one?" He asked for the fifth time, sipping from his cup. "Shape looks nice." Before we'd left the house, he'd pulled on a red flannel button-up that had hugged his biceps, as well as a pair of Wranglers that made my pussy weep.

Yeah, it was unfair how attractive he was. Especially when he topped it off with a Carhartt jacket, boots and cowboy hat.

I hadn't packed my entire wardrobe, but I'd grabbed my thick, fleece-lined tights, pairing them with my favorite turtle-neck sweater and skirt, throwing on a thick plaid pea coat overtop and a pair of pearl earrings. It felt like me. But somehow, it also felt like the old me. Like I was trying to be the girl that I'd been—the influencer who hundreds of thousands of people followed on social media, instead of just… Emily.

I paused for a moment, frowning at the blue spruce. "I don't know. It just doesn't feel right."

He just nodded, and we continued strolling along.

There were tons of varieties of trees on the lot—all kinds of firs, pines and spruces, but I was looking for the perfect one. Luckily, Mason didn't seem to care how long I took, wandering down the aisles. Maybe because this was our first time out in society in almost a week, neither of us was in a rush to go back inside. His buddy Jonah had been there when we'd gotten to the lot, patting Mason on the back before he officially introduced himself to me. It felt good to have him introduce me to his friends. Like he really was in this for the long haul.

"Emily?" A voice called out. Turning, I found Hannah and her husband, Anthony, all bundled up and walking towards us. He had their son, Brandon, strapped to his chest. Anthony was tall, at six feet. Not as tall as Mason, of course, who practically towered over my five-foot-nine. At six-four, he was a giant. In more ways than one.

"Hi, Han." I grinned. "Didn't expect to see you here." I looked up at Mason, who squeezed my hand. "You remember Mason, right?"

My best friend smiled at him. "Of course. How could I forget?" He quirked an eyebrow, and I just shook my head. "Mason, this is my best friend Hannah and her husband, Tony. And their little boy, Brandon."

"It's good to meet you both. Wow. Look at this little cutie, huh?" Mason said, grinning down at her baby. Brandon had brown eyes, just like Antony's. "How old is he?"

I could see in his eyes how badly he wanted that. He'd told me, but I hadn't felt the longing until now. God, this man would be an incredible father. I knew it just from the way he took care of me. I squeezed his hand, just letting him know I was there. That I saw him.

"Seven months," Hannah beamed, tugging on Brandon's tiny hat. "And thank you. We're both so obsessed with him." She booped his little button nose.

"Me too," I agreed. "I'm going to need more godmother time in the new year," I said to Hannah.

"So, you're staying?" She asked, looking between us expectantly.

Mason curled an arm around my hip almost possessively. My face flushed, and I was grateful for the cold that most definitely had already made the tip of my nose pink. "Um. Yeah. I don't have any travel plans anytime soon." Sure, I'd had offers, but I was burnt out. I didn't know what was next, but I was ready for something more… stable. "What are you two doing here? I thought you already had a tree?"

"We do," Anthony said, grinning down at his wife. "But after being cooped up with the storm for so many days, we thought some fresh air would do us some good, so we took a walk around downtown."

"And that's when we spotted you," Hannah added. "I was going to text you to make sure you were alive this afternoon anyway."

"Well, here we are." I knew she noticed how I said *we*, and I tried to hide my blush.

"So, you two are…" My best friend trailed off, waiting for me to finish her thought.

I looked up at Mason. "We're—"

"Together," he answered, no hesitation.

My heart swooned at the declaration. "Yeah," I confirmed, leaning into his side and squeezing his hand back. "We are." Not a label, but it was even better, somehow.

Hannah grinned. "How'd *that* happen?"

"Mason came to check on me when the snowstorm hit, and we sort of… hit it off, I guess." I looked at him, wondering if that was an adequate answer.

"Took one look at her in that bar and knew I had to make her mine," he confirmed.

"Mason," I said, blushing harder.

He dropped his lips, brushing them against my cheek. "What? It's true. Just had to get out of my head first."

Hannah just smiled. "Well, we'll leave you two lovebirds to it. Have fun picking out your tree."

We exchanged hugs, promising to hang out more after the new year, and then it was just Mason and me again. He interlaced his fingers through mine once more, pressing a kiss to the back of my hand.

"So, *together*, huh?"

Mason grinned. "Better get used to it, darlin'. Because I'm not lettin' go of you."

I stood on my tiptoes to press my lips against his. "Glad to hear it, cowboy."

And then I saw it. The perfect tree.

"That one," I told him, feeling giddy. It would look perfect in the living room. "What do you think?"

"Yeah," he answered. "Perfect." But when I looked back up at him, he wasn't looking at the tree. He was looking at *me*.

Mason squeezed my hand. "When we get back from dropping the tree off, I was thinking we could take the horses out for a ride."

I couldn't stop my answering grin. "Yes, please."

"God, it's really coming down out there," I observed, standing at the open door of the barn. "*Again.*" Apparently, this was just going to be our thing. Getting caught together in snowstorms. Secretly, I liked that we had a thing.

Mason clicked his tongue against the roof of his mouth, wrapping his arms around me. "Good thing we came inside when we did." Mason was all bundled up in his coat, wearing gloves and a dark green beanie.

We'd already stabled up our horses after our ride, brushing them both down and giving them a generous amount of hay to eat. Now we were just watching the snow fall outside as the sky grew dark.

The ride had been magical. There was just something about being on the back of a horse in weather like this. Montana was so beautiful, one reason I could never imagine ever leaving for good. I'd miss this place too much if I called somewhere else home.

He pressed a kiss on my forehead. "You okay if I go check on a few things?"

I nodded, wanting to use it as an excuse to explore. Wiggling out of my damp coat, I hung it on the hook. After we'd gotten back from our little date—and dropped the tree off at my parents' house, setting it in the living room—we'd come back here and changed before going out to greet our horses.

A thousand memories flooded through me as I wandered through the stables. I'd spent so much time here when I was younger. Growing up, Mrs. Elliott had taught me to ride. Sometimes, Mason had even taught me lessons, helping me up onto the young mare I learned to ride on. My parents had bought me Smokey when I was twelve, tired of my begging to have a horse, and had built the small stable on our property.

The Elliott's facilities were pristine, and the barn itself was warm, sheltered from the outside snow. One of their primary operations—besides running the guest ranch that brought them income throughout the year—was breeding and raising horses. I walked through the barn, seeing all the mares in their stalls. A few of them were heavily pregnant, and I expected there would be some foals coming in the next few months.

Giving a small whistle, I called over a beautiful palomino with a gorgeous golden coat. She stuck her head out of the stall, nuzzling into me like she was curious if I had anything for her. I pulled a sugar cube out of my pocket—I'd stolen a handful when we'd gotten inside—and then rubbed at her neck. "Such a sweet girl," I said. "Look at you. So pretty."

"Look who's talking," said the deep voice I'd gotten so used to.

Spinning in surprise, I turned to find Mason, a sexy smirk covering his devilishly handsome face. He rubbed his beard. "Having fun, baby?"

"Just keeping the horses company," I replied, batting my eyelashes.

He grinned. "I could think of someone else who could use the company."

My body heated at the suggestion. Truthfully, I was already about to combust. I'd been turned on since earlier. The sight of Mason tending to the horses while wearing that cowboy hat and tight red flannel was doing something to my insides.

"Yeah?" Biting my lip, I looked directly at him as I unwound my scarf from my neck. "And what *ideas* did you have, cowboy?"

"Emily." Mason's voice was rough. "Darlin'."

I took another step towards him, this time peeling my sweater from my body, letting it drop to the floor, exposing my dark green lacy bra that did nothing to hide my pebbled nipples.

Another step, and I flicked open the button of my jeans, kicking off my boots before pushing them down my thighs.

And then I stood in front of him, dressed only in my lingerie. My drawers were overflowing with matching sets—I wore them for me, because they made me feel pretty and feminine—but there was something about Mason's eyes as he raked them over my body that made me know it was *absolutely* worth it.

I stepped closer, running my hands up his chest, slowly popping each button on his flannel through the hole.

"Whatcha doin', baby?" He murmured, reaching out and weaving his fingers through my hair.

"Remember what you told me in the bar?" I asked, biting

my lip as I undid the last button, pushing his shirt down his shoulders.

"Uh-huh." His response scraped over my skin.

"Thought it was time to finally try it out." I pressed my lips against his ear. "You know. Riding my cowboy."

We both worked in tandem to pull his long-sleeved under-shirt over his head, baring his muscular chest, and that little happy trail of dark hair, to me. He slipped his fingers into the waistband of my panties, tugging on them, pulling me closer until we were pressed together, chest to chest. His hands wrapped around my back, unhooking my bra, letting it fall to the ground before he pushed my underwear down my hips, letting me shimmy them down my legs.

He let out a groan as I reached down for his belt, unbuck-ling it before pulling it out of his jeans. I shoved his pants—and boxer briefs—down his hips, letting him kick off his boots before pushing them the rest of the way off.

Mason tugged me back against him, and I placed my hand on his chest, pushing him back until we hit the wall, and then he slid down to the floor, keeping his back to the wall.

Climbing onto his lap, I ran my hands up his chest, running my fingers through his chest hair, before they landed on his biceps. "So, what do you say, Mason?"

His eyes flared with heat as he took me in. My nipples, hard and aching for his touch. My pussy positioned directly over his cock. And even though he'd let me take control, I knew who really held all the power here.

"You're forgetting something," he said, clicking his tongue against the roof of his mouth.

"Hm?" I fluttered my eyelashes at him as I ground down on his thick length. I already couldn't wait to have it inside me.

He took his hat off his head and placed it on mine. "You gotta wear the hat, baby."

I adjusted the way it sat on my head, tilting the brim up so I could still kiss him.

"Come on, cowgirl," he said, holding my hips. "Ride me."

Raising my hips, I guided his tip to my entrance, sinking down on it slowly. I was so wet, I didn't need any foreplay before having him inside of me. The anticipation all day had made this even better, somehow. He was so big—long and thick, with a girth that made me stretch around him no matter how prepared I was.

Wiggling my way down, I worked inch after inch of his cock inside of me, until I'd taken every inch. I started off slow, rocking my hips back and forth, each movement grinding my clit down against the base of his shaft.

His lips found my neck, kissing and sucking on my skin as I brought my knees closer together, using them as leverage to slide up and down on his thick length.

"Use me, Darlin'. I can take it." He tugged at my earlobe with his teeth. He propped up his knees, supporting me with his thighs, and bounced me on his cock. His hands—still gripping my hips—helped guide them as I kept up the slow, torturous pace.

I let out a moan as he thrust his hips up, burying himself inside of me, and continued grinding down on him, the position too much. I was stuffed full of him, my arousal practically dripping down his hard cock.

He was hot and hard as steel inside of me as I rode him, rolling my hips, chasing my orgasm.

"That's it," he praised, his hands cupping my breasts, flicking over my nipples. "That's my good girl. Take it. Take what you need from me."

"Mason," I panted, crying out as he leaned his head forward, capturing a nipple with his mouth. "It's too much. I feel so—" Tears pooled in my eyes from the pleasure overwhelming my body. "It's too good."

"You're doing so good, cowgirl." He took over for me, somehow finding the exact rhythm to make me shatter, my orgasm hitting me hard and fast. I slumped against his chest, and he wrapped his arms around me, one pressed to my lower back and the other around my neck as he cradled me to his body. His hat had fallen off my head at some point, falling onto the floor next to me.

He was still hard inside of me, his crown pressed against my cervix, cock throbbing as he whispered sweet nothings into my ear, rubbing my back in slow, soothing circles.

When I finally came back to myself, I realized he still hadn't come.

"Mason—" I started.

"Shhh." He smoothed a piece of hair back behind my ear. "That was for you. We can take care of me later."

"But…" I pouted. "I wanted you to come inside me."

He groaned. "That's my greedy little cumslut, huh? You want to have me leaking out of you as we walk home? My cum trailing down your thighs, so you know who you belong to?"

I nodded. I'd gotten addicted to the feeling of him filling me up, of his warmth flooding my insides.

"Yes," I moaned. "I want it."

He flipped us over so I was on my back, and he was positioned on top of me, his body wedged between my thighs. He was wound so tight that I wasn't sure how he was still holding on. The veins in his arms practically popped out as he braced himself over me.

"This what you want, huh?" he asked, dropping his lips to mine as he thrust in earnest between my thighs. It wouldn't take much for me to orgasm again—I could already feel it building inside of me. "Needy girl wants to get bred." He paused, his eyes widening for a moment, as if the words shocked him.

I couldn't hold back my moan. While the words should have freaked me out, they had the exact opposite effect. I was hot all over, biting my lip as I considered the idea. Why was the thought of Mason getting me pregnant so *hot?*

Maybe not now. But it was hard not to picture it.

He grunted, his thumb finding my clit and rubbing it as he pumped his cock into my pussy. It was obvious with each thrust just how wet I was, the squelching noises filling the space as our bodies came together, over and over again.

"*Mason.*" I cried his name. "Please. Give me your cum."

And as he spilled inside of me—the light snow still coming down outside—I couldn't help but think that if he knocked me up, I wouldn't even be mad.

14
mason

 ou seem happy," my dad commented as I finished up my work, sliding my chair underneath my desk. "This have anything to do with the girl your mother was telling me about? The Sullivan's daughter?"

I ran my fingers through my hair. Of course, she'd told him. I shouldn't have been surprised.

"Maybe," I murmured, looking out the window.

I'd come home to Emily every single night since she'd come with me, and yeah—it had been damn hard to wipe the smile off my face these days. We'd brought her car back, too, so she could come and go from my cabin, letting her head home and water all of her mom's plants and check on her parents' house when she needed to.

But at night, she was in my bed. And every morning, I gave her a kiss before I slid out of bed, heading out to the ranch to take care of things. I wanted every day to be just like this last week had been. To be together, whatever that looked like.

She told Hannah that she wasn't planning on going

anywhere anytime soon. Did that mean she wanted to stay here with me? I sure as fuck hoped so.

And then, afterwards, she'd blown my mind by riding me in the barn.

"I just want you to follow your heart, son." My dad clasped his hand on my shoulder. "That's all your mom and I have ever wanted from you. For you to be happy. To have the life you want."

"I know." I was all choked up. "I feel like I wasted so much time on the wrong woman when the right one was here all along." I shook my head.

"So don't let her go."

"It's not that simple."

"Isn't it?" He winked. "If I know you—and I do—I know you'll give that girl everything. But just make sure that she'll give *you* everything too, okay?"

I nodded. "Yeah, Dad." I looked outside. "I should go."

"Bring her by the house soon," he told me as I grabbed my coat and slipped it on. "Your mother and I would like to say hi."

I chuckled. "Will do."

Waving goodbye to my dad, I headed outside, eager to head home—back to Emily.

Back to the girl I hadn't been able to get my mind off of from that first night in the bar.

Was it because I'd known, even then, that she was the one for me? Somehow, in the back of my mind, I knew it was true. What would have happened if I'd kissed her then? If I hadn't been stupid, trying to deny my attraction to her because she was Hunter's little sister?

She might have been eight years younger than me, but did that really matter in the grand scheme of things? No, we were both adults. As long as we both wanted the same thing—and I was pretty sure we did, especially after the way she'd reacted when I'd accidentally let it slip that I had a slight breeding kink when it came to her. The thought had my cock twitching in my pants, more eager than ever to go find the girl who I was pretty sure was my forever.

"What are we doing here?" Emily frowned as I shut off the truck, pulling up outside of *Giddy Up.* After I'd got home from a long day of work, I'd told her we were going out, and to put on something that made her feel pretty. Em had dressed up in a tight plaid skirt, a long-sleeved top that hugged her tits in all the best ways, and a pair of cowgirl boots.

My hand slid up her bare thigh. I was trying hard not to ask whether she had any panties on underneath it. Lately, more often than not, she wasn't wearing any when I got home, leaving me free to pick her up and eat her out on the counter or fuck her on the kitchen table. Plenty of times, we'd been so desperate for each other that we hadn't left the couch. It was fucking incredible.

I squeezed her leg. "Havin' a do-over, darlin'."

She laughed. "Why?"

"Because," I frowned. "That first night, I fucked up. I knew you wanted to kiss me, and I pushed you away, thinking that this could never work between us."

She took the hand that was still on her leg and interlaced her fingers with mine, not saying anything. Like somehow, she knew I needed to get this out.

"I should have kissed you right then and there. Should have carried you out the door and taken you home with me. Brought you to my bed and never let you leave. Because, Emmie Girl, I took one look at you, standing there so gorgeous at the bar, and I knew that if I let myself, you'd be my entire future."

Emily let out a small whimper. I picked up our combined hands, kissing the back of hers.

"So I want a re-do of that night. One where I see you, and I'm not a coward. Where I buy you a drink, and then ask you to dance, and at the end of the night, I'm still the lucky bastard you decide to go home with."

She nodded. "Okay."

Leaning over, I brushed my lips over hers. "Stay here." Climbing out of my truck, I walked around, opening her door. Just like when I'd taken her to my cabin, I wrapped my hands around her much smaller waist, lifting her out of the truck and setting her down on her feet. She reached up, adjusting the hat on my head and gave me a small smile. "Let's do this, cowboy."

"You go in first," I told her. "Wait for me at the bar."

She fluttered her eyelashes. "Only if you promise not to make me wait for too long."

Fuck. My little vixen. I couldn't help but drop another kiss to her lips. "Of course not, baby." I gave her a soft slap on the ass. "Now go be a good girl and wait for your cowboy to find you."

She gave me a cheeky smile as she disappeared inside. I looked up at the sky, praying to whatever God was listening for the ability to make it through the night.

"You here alone, darlin'?" I rasped against her ear, wrapping an arm around her waist just like I'd done that first night— before I'd realized it was Emily in my arms.

She turned around, giving me a coy look. "I was waiting for someone, but he didn't show."

"Bummer. Guess his loss is my gain, huh?" I let my hand drape possessively over her back.

"What brings you here tonight?"

"Looking for the prettiest girl in town."

Her fingers danced over the top of the wooden bar. "And… did you find her?"

"I did." She was standing in front of me, those long as fuck legs somehow even sexier thanks to those boots that I wanted wrapped around my waist as I fucked her later.

She smiled, those green eyes sparkling even in the low light. "So, are you gonna buy me a drink, cowboy?"

"Sure am." I flagged over the bartender, ordering her a cocktail—what she'd been drinking that first night—and a beer on tap for me.

When we had our drinks in hand, we drifted over to one of the high top tables.

She smiled at me over the rim of her drink as she took a sip. "Mmm." She swiped her tongue over her lips. "Sweet."

"Glad you like it," I said, taking a long pull of my beer.

"I do." She took another drink. "How'd you know what I wanted?"

I flashed her a smile. "Maybe I've been watchin' you, beautiful. Waiting until you were all alone to swoop in and have you for myself."

Her eyes heated, snagging on my arms where I'd rolled up my shirt. This last week, I'd learned that forearm porn—whatever the fuck that was—really did it for her. Apparently, she enjoyed seeing my shirt rolled up over my thick, muscular arms. I'd pulled out the big guns tonight, hoping she'd be aroused and needy from my attention. This role-play was *fun*—like a precursor to everything we knew was going to happen tonight.

The whole thing was like foreplay, and I was fucking obsessed.

"Yeah? So, what can I call you, cowboy?" Emily tucked a strand of wavy brown hair behind her ear.

"Mason," I told her, wanting to hear it from her perfect lips. "The name's Mason Elliott."

"I'm Emily Sullivan." She swirled the drink in her glass, giving me an appraising look, letting them linger on my pants for a beat longer than should have been acceptable. My dick practically leapt in my pants at the attention, twitching at the thought of her interest. "You know what they say about a cowboy with a large belt buckle…"

I grinned as I tried to calm my cock down. I let my fingers trail up her bare thigh. Two could play this game. "You know what they say. Save a horse…" I winked. "Ride a cowboy."

She laughed, and God, when was the last time I'd let loose like this? When was the last time I'd felt so light and *happy?* My dad was right. And it was all because of Emily. Because over the last two weeks, she'd changed me for the better. She'd shown me what life could be like if I opened up my heart again.

And goddamn, did I love her. Fast? Maybe.

But I knew she was my forever girl. And if I didn't think it was too soon, I'd get down on one knee right here, right now, and ask her to be my bride. To marry me. To be my wife and the mother of my children. Because I wanted all of that with her. A life—a family.

She leaned in real close, standing on her tiptoes to press her lips against my ear. "You can ride me all night, cowboy."

"Is that a promise?" I wrapped my hands around her waist.

Emily hummed in response, tilting up her face towards mine. Her lips looked so soft—pretty pink pillows that begged to be kissed. I wanted to kiss her all over—her mouth, her tits, between her thighs. Maybe later, if she let me, I'd spend the night worshiping her there, burying my tongue inside her cunt.

I shook my head. I was getting ahead of myself.

A slow song came on, and Emily's eyes fluttered shut, a radiant smile spreading over her face. There was a live band tonight, playing popular country songs. Mostly love songs, but I wasn't complaining. They all felt a little too accurate right now. Because my feelings were bursting through me, not caring if it was too soon or that we'd barely been together.

"Oh, I love this song," she murmured, softly signing the lyrics to *you look like you love me*.

I stuck my hand out for her, setting my drink down on the bar. "Emily, would you care to dance?"

Her eyes sparkled as she looked up at me, sliding her palm into mine. "Thought you'd never ask, Mason."

I held her hand as we wandered out onto the dance floor, her hand sliding onto my shoulder as I wrapped mine around her waist, keeping her pressed tight against me. We kept our other hands interlaced as we swayed to the music, content to just hold each other.

"You were right," she finally murmured after the first song had bled into the second and we hadn't moved.

I held up my arm to spin her, and her cheeks were flushed with excitement as I pulled her back into my arms. "About what?" I asked, dropping my lips to her ear.

"Our do-over. This is nice."

"Mmm." I pressed my forehead against hers. "It's still missin' something, though."

She looked up at me through her eyelashes. "What?"

"Told you I regretted not kissin' you that night. I'm not gonna make that mistake again." I cupped her cheek, lowering my lips till they brushed over hers. "So tell me, cowgirl."

Emily's tongue darted out, moistening her lower lip. "Tell you what?"

"Tell me you want to be kissed."

She smiled. "Will you kiss me, cowboy?"

"I thought you'd never ask." I lowered my lips to hers, pressing a soft kiss on her lips. In this moment, I didn't notice any of the other couples around us on the dance floor. Everything else went quiet, and it was just her and I. She opened for me, and I slid my tongue against hers, savoring the sweet and sour taste of her drink on her tongue.

She smiled up at me as we pulled apart, and my heart skipped a beat in my chest. God, she was beautiful. This gorgeous, amazing woman was all mine. And I'd do whatever it took to keep her. The last week had shown me exactly how good we could be together, and there was no way I was giving up on that.

I dipped my head against her ear as I spun her. "I'm just a cowboy looking for the right cowgirl, and I think I've found her." I let my hand drift down to her ass.

She blushed. "Mason…"

"Mhm?"

Emily reached up, pressing her fingers against my jaw, rubbing at my stubble. "Take me home."

I didn't even need to hesitate. "With pleasure."

15
emily

$\mathcal{E}$ven though I loved Mason's cozy cabin, we were snuggled up on the couch at my parents' house on Christmas Eve. He'd asked me to stay with him until Christmas, but it just felt right being *home* for the holiday. We'd already agreed to spend tomorrow night with his parents, and it was strange how easy everything felt so completely normal.

Like I wasn't going to his family's house as his girlfriend for the first time.

The last week with him had been like a lens into what our life could look like together, and I wanted it so desperately. After our do-over night at the bar—where he'd kissed me passionately on the dance floor, not caring who saw—I knew that this was something *more*. It was obvious, when he'd taken me home, laid me in his bed, and buried his face between my thighs, making me come twice on his mouth and once on his fingers before he'd ever slid inside of me, fucking me slow and sweet. It was tender, the way he made love to me, and I'd almost blurted out how I felt right then and there.

We talked about nothing and everything—what we liked, what we hated, our hopes and dreams for the future. The way I'd been thinking about what came next for me. That I loved traveling, but I wanted something of my own. Something more. I didn't know what it was yet, but Mason was sure I'd find it.

We hadn't shared our feelings yet, but I knew what I felt.

I couldn't help but snuggle against his chest as we watched the fire flicker. The tree was decked out in lights— and all of my family's ornaments. Mason had started the fire in the fireplace when we'd arrived, and we didn't bother turning the lights on, letting the glow from both illuminate the room, making everything feel so cozy and perfect.

"I can't believe it's almost Christmas," I told him. "It feels like I blinked, and the two weeks are over." My parents landed the day after tomorrow, and then I'd go back to living in their basement like nothing had ever happened. Unless Mason asked me to stay with him.

Secretly, I wanted that. To move my things into the free closet in his cabin. The master had two walk-ins, and the second one felt like it had just been waiting for me. No other woman had ever slept in his bed or spent the night in the house with him. He'd confessed that to me the second night with his body curled around mine.

I still got warm thinking about what that meant. That he'd chosen *me.*

"Why are you blushing?" Mason traced my cheek.

I shook my head. "Not important."

He leaned over me until my back hit the couch, and he propped himself up on top of me. My thighs fell apart, letting him straddle me. "Tell me." He pressed his erection into my core, and I let out a small whine. He knew exactly what he was doing to me.

Covering my face with my hands, I whispered, "I still can't believe that we're here. That you want *me*. Me, the girl who was obsessed with you as a kid. Your best friend's little sister."

He leaned down, pressing a kiss to my cheek. "Well, you better get used to it, baby. Because I'm not going anywhere. You're stuck with me." Mason kissed me, rubbing his hard bulge against my entrance and making me ready to beg for him to put it inside of me, when the doorbell rang.

"*Why?*" I cried out, letting my head fall back against the couch. "Maybe if we ignore them, they'll go away." I pressed my lips to his mouth again, not wanting to interrupt this. It was hard to keep my hands off this man.

He frowned, his brow furrowing. I wanted to smooth it with my thumb. "Maybe we should check to see who it is. I can't think of who would be here at this hour."

Mason was right. It was getting late, and the only people I could think of who might be there—like Hannah and her husband, my parents, or his—all would have called first.

Last night, we'd gone over to his parents' house for dinner. He'd finally stopped monopolizing my time and shared me with them, and they'd clearly been ecstatic to see their only son so happy. I'd known them both since I was a baby, and Mason's mom was the warm, welcoming mom that I always wished mine had been.

But when I opened the door, it was none of those people standing at the front door. "What are you doing here?" I blinked a few times, but they were all still standing in front of me.

My brothers—Hunter and Benjamin—and their wives and kids were all here. At my parents' door. Holding armfuls of presents and wearing silly Christmas pajamas. Plus Hunter and Gabbi's dog Rowan, who barked excitedly at me as she tugged on the leash in Hunter's hand, eager to say hi.

There was no stopping my eyes from filling with tears.

"I thought you guys couldn't make it," I said, choked up. "Mom said…" I shook my head.

"Hey." My older brother grinned.

Mason's deep voice called out, "Who's there?" He walked towards the door, wrapping an arm around my waist before freezing as he realized who, exactly, was standing on the porch.

Hunter's eyes widened. "Mason? You two…"

It was pretty obvious *why* he was here, considering he was wearing flannel pajama bottoms—and no shirt. And then there was the fact that I was wearing *his* t-shirt. Thank God I actually had panties on this time—and a pair of Christmas horse fleece pajama bottoms. I'd never have heard the end of it from either of my brothers if I'd opened the door in just a shirt.

"Um… surprise?" I let out a nervous laugh.

"Alright boys." Angelina pushed inside, carrying one twin on her hip. "You all figure that out. I'm going inside where it's warm. Hi, Emily." She gave me a one-armed hug. Gabbi followed behind her, holding my niece, and did the same.

"Hi, you guys." I looked at the whole family as they stood right inside the door. "I can't… Why are you here? Weren't you spending Christmas in Portland?"

"We came to spend Christmas with *you*, Em," Benjamin said, still holding the other twin in his arms. They were identical, so it was still hard to keep them straight. Luckily, they'd started dressing Zachary in red, and Wesley in blue from the time they were infants. It was the only way I could keep them straight. Apparently, one of them had a freckle behind their ear that could help you tell, but I wouldn't rely on that.

"Mom didn't want you to be alone," Hunter added.

"Oh. Well, that was nice of you."

"She didn't tell you?" Benjamin frowned.

I shook my head. "I've only talked to her a few times since she left, though, what with the snowstorm and all." I looked back at Mason. He just gave me a small smile. Did he know? Had he done this somehow? Knowing that I was missing my family, he… brought me my brothers?

My oldest brother gave us both a pointed look. "Clearly, you're *not* alone, though, so…"

Mason winced. "I'm sorry, Hunt. We were going to tell you."

He waved us off. "I'm not upset."

"You're not?"

Hunter shrugged. "You're an adult. I trust the choices you want to make. And if that choice is Mason, well…" He stuck out his hand for Mason to shake it. "I know he's a good man."

My oldest brother nodded to him. "Make her happy, alright?"

My cowboy looked at me, nodding his head. "I didn't plan on anything less."

I felt my cheeks warm all over again. Sometimes it felt like he existed just to make me happy. But it wasn't just about that. I wanted to make him happy, too. Wanted him to have everything he'd ever wanted.

"So, he's your boyfriend?" Angelina asked with one arm propped on her hip.

"Damn right I am," he responded, not giving me a chance. He pressed a kiss onto my cheek.

Mason, my *boyfriend*. It was a little strange, given he was thirty-six and very much a *man*, calling him my boyfriend, but it felt right.

We all moved into the living room. Gabbi and Angelina set their babies on the rug, and I crawled down beside them, soaking up a few moments with my precious niece and nephews. God, they were adorable. I picked Quin up in my arms, raising her up and making plane noises, making her giggle with delight.

"I can't believe you guys are all here," I said, smiling at the chubby-cheeked baby girl in my arms, whose fist had captured a strand of my hair. She tugged on it, and I tried to pry it free, not wanting her to tear it out of my head.

"It wouldn't be Christmas without you, Em," Gabbi said, grinning. She and I had become friends after Angelina and Benjamin's joint bachelor and bachelorette trip the summer they'd gotten married. Hunter and Gabbi had planned the trip as best man and maid of honor, which had also been how they'd fallen in love. They'd tried to sneak around behind everyone's backs at first, finally coming clean during breakfast the morning after the wedding before they set off on a European vacation together.

It was something out of a romance novel. Angelina and Benjamin's story felt like that too. The two of them had a bit of a whirlwind relationship—they'd started dating in the fall, gotten engaged in the spring, and then had planned their wedding for that summer, in *France*. It was all wildly romantic, since Angelina's favorite city was Paris. I loved seeing my brother so besotted with a girl. Especially considering when they'd first met, she'd *hated* him. They'd been stuck together at a work retreat, though, and apparently, love and hate were two sides of the same coin. That was a story for a different time, though.

Still, I remembered the first time Ben had brought her home for his thirtieth birthday—over five years ago. We'd instantly bonded, and I was so excited to have another girl around after only ever having brothers. Now they had twin boys, who were rolling around on the floor, playing with toy cars that Angelina must have brought in with her.

We stayed like that for a while—us girls on the floor,

talking about the babies, plus what they'd been up to lately with Noelle and Charlotte, their other two best friends. Rowan was curled up at Gabbi's feet, giving her big puppy dog eyes as she got plenty of pets. Meanwhile, the guys were all piled on the couches, having their own conversation.

I looked over at the couch at my *boyfriend*. That still felt weird to say. I caught Mason's eyes fill with longing as he watched me hold Quinlan. He was talking to Hunter and Ben, catching up, but he couldn't look away from me. He hadn't brought up the idea of getting me pregnant again since the barn, but I knew he wanted kids. There was a desire in his gaze that I didn't think I was imagining.

Gabbi yawned, and then my oldest brother was off the couch, heaving his wife into his arms before scooping Quinlan up from me. "It was a long drive," he told us. "I'm going to take my girls to bed. See you in the morning?"

I nodded. "Night, Hunt. Night, Gabs." I blew Quinlan a kiss. "Night, baby Quinny."

"We should go to bed, too," Benjamin said, kneeling in front of his wife. "You got Z?"

She nodded, heaving Zachary up into her arms. I gave both twins a kiss on the forehead, and then Benjamin picked up Wesley.

"Night, you two," my brother said, sliding his hand into Ang's. The two of them each had a twin on their front, clinging to them like a koala. "Don't stay up too late."

I shook my head. "We won't." Honestly, I could already feel sleep pulling down my eyelids.

It was Mason's turn to bend down, scooping me up into his arms. "I can walk, you know," I protested. But honestly, as he carried me down the stairs, it felt so similar to those beginning days we'd spent here, all alone in our own world as the storm raged on outside.

"For old time's sake," he told me, kissing my cheek.

I gave a little sigh, but I didn't protest any further. Not when this was the only place I wanted to be in the world.

Creeping up the stairs, I slipped into the living room, laid out a blanket and sat in front of the fireplace. The fire had long since burned out, leaving only the embers behind the screen, but no one had bothered to unplug the tree.

I hadn't bothered. I loved the lights. Loved staring at the ornaments my family had collected over the years. They all had sentimental value. My mom loved putting up a giant tree in the entryway—decked out beautifully, like it came straight from a magazine, but the one in the living room was always our family tree.

It had a reindeer made of popsicle sticks that I'd made in elementary school. Little clay Santas that were made of all three of our handprints. It was our life up there. Family vacations—the ones we'd taken, at least, since my parents had always been working.

When I was younger, this had been my tradition. I'd sneak downstairs, sit on the couch, staring at the tree as I waited for Santa. I'd fight to keep my eyes open as long as possible until I finally succumbed to sleep. And every time, without fail, I'd wake up to a tree full of presents.

Wrapping my arms around my legs, I watched as the lights flickered. It was late—past midnight—which meant it was officially Christmas Day. My brothers and their wives had long since gone to bed, both of them taking their old rooms. Sometime between then and now, a few dozen presents had appeared underneath the tree.

I couldn't help but imagine my future like this. One where

the kids toddling through the living room were mine. With dark hair and dark blue eyes and little cowboy hats.

My heart ached just thinking about Mason's ex and how heartbroken he'd been, knowing she'd changed her mind about kids. There was nothing wrong with it, but I hated that he had ever had to go through that pain.

Still, I was grateful to her. Because she gave me him.

I'd left Mason in my bed, shirtless and ridiculously sexy. The perfect Christmas present. The only thing that would make it better is if I got to unwrap *him* in the morning. I smiled at the idea. On second thought, I could probably make that happen.

"Can't sleep?" A deep voice called out. I turned to find my cowboy walking up the stairs, dressed in his ridiculous Christmas pajamas.

I shook my head as he squeezed my shoulder. "No. Just thinking." About the future. About how much I cared about the man at my side. My feelings had grown so much, it was hard to hold them back.

"Good. I wanted to give you your present. Hold on." He reached behind the tree, pulling out a fairly large box. I hadn't even noticed it earlier.

"What is this?" My eyes were wide as he placed it in my lap. "When did you even have time to get me something?"

"Just…" he scratched the back of his head. "Just open it, please, baby?"

I couldn't deny him anything, not when he asked me with that voice. I pulled at the paper, running my fingernail through the tape to pop it off, trying not to rip it.

He chuckled. "I have more paper if you're worried about ruining it."

"Oh. I just…" I shook my head, finally just tearing it off. After exposing the box underneath, I cut the tape—though I'd needed scissors this time—and gasped as I opened the box.

I pulled out a few sheets of tissue paper, but there was no mistaking it.

"You bought me a hat?"

He nodded. "Your very own cowgirl hat. Felt necessary if you're gonna be a real workin' cowgirl on the ranch. Y'know… if you want that." He looked hopeful, and butterflies erupted in my chest.

I sniffled. "I love it." *I loved him.* So much. My eyes watered, but I blinked the tears back.

Mason's hand wrapped around my neck, bringing our lips together. He kissed me softly, his lips moving against mine in a way that had me melting against his body.

"And I do, I think. Want to help at the ranch. In case you didn't know, I'm pretty good at social media. And I've always loved horses." I'd never be a breeder or a trainer, but I was happy to do what I could.

He pinched my ass. "You're hired."

I giggled, and then straightened, turning to look at him fully. I bit my lip. "So… does this position come with room and board? Cause I was thinking that *maybe,* it's time for me to move out of my parent's basement." I *really* didn't want to turn thirty and still have to tell people around town that I lived with my parents. God, I hated the judgement.

And I might have wanted a bit of privacy, considering I had gotten used to having regular sex with the cowboy who seemed all too happy to satisfy my every need.

Mason stilled, his eyes scanning my face, like he was trying to decide if I was serious. "Really? You want to move in with me? Like… permanently?"

"Yes? God, is that crazy?" I shook my head. "Maybe we need to slow down. I don't know." I let out a weak laugh. "I've never done this before. But yeah. I want to. If you… want me to."

He hauled me onto his lap, practically mauling me with

more kisses. "*Please* move in," he begged. "After spending the last two weeks sharing a bed with you, I don't think I could sleep apart from you if I tried."

"Are you sure?" My eyes were watery.

He nodded. "I was gonna ask, but I didn't want to make a mess of things. God knows I fucked things up at the beginning. So I was trying to be patient. Wait at least a month or two." Mason laughed, tucking a piece of hair behind my ear.

"I don't want to be apart from you," I admitted. "This Christmas was…" I didn't even have words to describe how amazing it had been. "It was more than I could have ever expected. More than I imagined. But even if I had to do it all over again, I wouldn't change anything." I loved our story. "Sure, it took a little snow to bring us together, but I like to think that was the universe—if not the good state of Montana —trying to get us together."

"A little?" He laughed. "Same, darlin'. And now, all I want is to spend every Christmas with you from now on. Together. I know we haven't talked about the future, but bein' with you…" Mason cupped my cheek, stroking his thumb over my skin. "That's all I want."

"Mason…" I whispered.

"I love you," he told me, cupping the back of my neck. "And I know it's fast, but I do. God help me, Emily, I do. It hit me like a snowstorm, you know. But there you were—so beautiful and breathtaking and everything I've ever wanted. So fucking perfect, and all I could do was want you. But now I have you, and all I can think is that I never want to let you go. That if there's any chance that I can keep you, I have to take it." He leaned forward, pressing our foreheads together. "I know I have some baggage, but if you'll have me—"

"I love you too," I said, no longer second-guessing if it was too soon. So what if people thought we'd fallen in love fast? I'd known him my entire life. He'd always been there. I didn't have to second-guess this decision. Not when I'd spent the past two weeks falling in love with him. Watching him.

"I want that too," I whispered. "All of it."

He smiled against my lips. "Then it's settled. You're livin' with me. Whatever you need, baby, whatever you want, I'll give it to you. You want the moon? I'll lasso it down for you."

I laughed, a wet sound because I was crying, too. "What about a cow?"

He frowned. "You want a *cow*?"

"Have you *seen* those cute baby Highland cows? They're adorable."

"Alright. Guess we're going to be cow parents," he grumbled.

I laughed. "Just the hat is enough, Mase. I don't need anything else. Just you." I bit my lip. "At least, for now…" Looking up at him through my eyelashes, I gave him a small smile.

There was a chance I'd never seen Mason this happy before. Maybe the other day, when we'd ridden side by side on the backs of our horses through the Montana wilderness— that seemed pretty close. But this?

He took my breath away.

Mason rolled me onto my back, running his hand down my cheek. I widened my legs, allowing him to settle himself between them. "You know, earlier, I couldn't help but notice how good you looked, holding a baby in your arms."

"You like that, cowboy?" I couldn't help but rub myself against him.

"Fuck," he groaned. "Yes. I can't stop thinking about it. Makes me want to give you my baby."

I wrapped my legs around his waist, needing him closer. "I'm still on birth control, you know. Which is probably good, considering how much you've come inside of me." I rubbed one of my feet up his back as I latched my lips onto his neck.

He let out a rough groan. "Em. I can't fuck you here on the carpet with your brothers upstairs."

I pouted at him. "Then take me to bed, Mason. We can try as much as we want now, you know."

"But you want 'em?"

"Kids?" I clarified.

My cowboy nodded. "Yes. You know how I feel. I've always wanted a few kids running around this place. And I just can't help but hope…"

"I want kids too," I told him, practically beaming. "Maybe a ring first, but we have time."

"Fuck, woman," he groaned. "I'd marry you tomorrow if you let me."

"Baby steps, cowboy." I kissed his cheek. "For now, you've got me."

He climbed off of me and then pulled me into his arms, slowly swaying us back and forth against the carpet. "Merry Christmas, darlin'. You're the best gift I could have ever asked for."

"And just think, I didn't even have to wrap myself up in a bow." I grinned.

He pretended to think about it. "No… but after your brothers leave, I think you should show me… just in case." Mason smirked.

I laughed. "Merry Christmas, Mason. I love you."

And then… there weren't any more words.

Not as we walked downstairs together—hand in hand. Not as we stripped out of our clothes, losing ourselves in each other.

No words as we made love to each other in the quiet darkness of the early morning.

We didn't need them.

Because I loved him, and he loved me. Everything else was inconsequential.

We still had a lot of things to figure out. A lot of growing that we'd do together, because this was still new. But I knew that no matter what happened, no matter what life threw my way, I'd never stop wanting this cowboy to be mine.

And he was mine.

Perfectly, effortlessly, *merrily* mine.

16
emily

Christmas Day had always been one of my favorite days of the year. Waking up in the morning, spending the entire day with my parents—who actually kept their promise and didn't work—and opening presents together was one tradition I loved the most from childhood. This year, it was even better.

Maybe because I'd never had a boyfriend to spend Christmas with before. The idea still made me giddy. I smiled, thinking about last night. *He loved me.*

Part of me still couldn't believe it, even as I woke up curled around him. That of all the people in the universe, somehow they'd given me this man. My childhood crush. My brother's best friend. And now he was simply just *mine.* My cowboy, my Mason. My future.

I left him sleeping in my bed—he needed it, especially after how late we'd stayed up last night—and crept upstairs to start some coffee. Wrapping myself up in a blanket, I went to sit outside on the hanging porch swing my parents had installed years ago. Part of me had always loved sitting on the deck just like this and looking out over the vast Montana wilderness. The perk of our house sitting on a giant plot of land: there wasn't another house for miles. The Elliotts were our closest neighbors, and unlike in the city, there was a stillness to the land here.It was beautiful and peaceful in a way I couldn't get over.

Of course, Mason's cabin was like this too. I felt a serene tranquility here that I wasn't sure I'd found anywhere else in the world. A sense of calm I'd never felt anywhere else. Hundreds of brand trips later, and still, the place I loved the most was right here.

Home.

Though that word had a new meaning now. Home wasn't just my parents or my brothers. It was Montana. It was on Smokey's back, riding through the pine trees and breathing in the fresh air. It was in the little A-frame cabin I was slowly becoming obsessed with. It was in the smile of the cowboy I'd fallen for. In the arms of the man I loved.

I knew no matter where I went—no matter what house I lived in—Mason would be my home now.

The porch creaked behind me, and I turned, not surprised at all to find my brothers standing there, both wearing pajama bottoms and sweatshirts.

Ben's were Batman themed, to no one's surprise—the man loved his comic books—while Hunter's were a green plaid pattern. My oldest brother had his sleeves pushed up, exposing his sleeves of tattoos, including the trees that adorned one of his arms, and the tributes to the patients he lost on the other.

Trees that reminded him of home. I'd never gotten a tattoo, wanting to make sure if I ever did, it was something meaningful, but I'd been thinking more about it lately. About what I'd get, how I could permanently mark my skin with the things I loved.

"Merry Christmas, Emily," Benjamin said.

"Hey." I smiled as they sat down on either side of me. "Good morning."

"Didn't know you'd be awake this early." Hunter chuckled, reaching over and rubbing the top of my head, messing up my hair.

I swatted his hand away. *"Hunter,"* I groaned. "Guess I was too excited. You know me."

Benjamin nodded. "You were always awake at six am, ready to open presents. I remember you literally dragging our parents out of bed one year."

Hunter snorted. "Don't forget her staying up as late as possible, trying to catch Santa. Can't forget all the years I carried you to bed, Em."

I blushed, not wanting to elaborate on how I'd done the same last night. Only this time, my wish had come true. I hadn't even needed Santa to show up. All I'd needed was my cowboy. "Well, you know what they say. Old habits die hard." I stared down at my coffee, sipping it slowly. It needed more whipped cream and flavoring. Somehow, I'd already gotten used to how Mason made it.

"Are you happy?" Hunter nudged me with his elbow.

I blinked up at him. "Huh?

"Tell me, sis. With Mason. Does he make you happy?"

Blushing, I nodded. "The happiest. I never knew…" I trailed off, then shook my head. "I just never knew what it was like to feel this happy. To… love someone like this. To feel so much. He's the love of my life, you know? And I know he was your best friend, but Mason really fought it, you know. He tried to stay away from me."

"You don't need my permission, you know," Hunter told me.

I sighed. "I know. But I don't want you to think it's weird, either. It just sort of… happened. We ran into each other at the bar, and then when the snowstorm hit…" I looked down at my slippered feet. "He came to check on me. And then he kinda got snowed in with me for the next few days. One thing led to another and…"

Benjamin shook his head, interrupting me. "Don't need any more details, Em. I'm begging you."

I shot him a pointed glare. "Tell that to your wife." There was no telling what Angelina would say at any given time. She was a black cat in every definition, but despite her and Ben fighting all the time, I knew how much they loved each other. Even if she had cursed him every day when she was pregnant with the twins.

"Oh, God. Please, no." He hung his head.

Hunter laughed. "I think we can all agree we do *not* need to share details of our sex lives." He screwed up his face.

It was nice to be like this. For so long, my brothers had barely talked to each other, but over the last five years, they'd become best friends again. Considering their wives were also best friends, it made sense.

"You're a doctor, Hunt." Benjamin rolled his eyes.

"A *pediatric* doctor. I work with kids." He glared at our brother.

I shoved them both, and we all grew quiet.

"If you're happy, Emily, that's all we ever wanted for our baby sister." Hunter squeezed my shoulder.

"Don't make me cry," I said, wiping underneath my eyes. "It's too early in the morning for that."

Benjamin chuckled. "We'll always have your back. And if he hurts you, he'll have to deal with both of us."

I sniffled. "Thank you."

"He's a good guy, though," Hunter said. "Sure, it might have been a shock at first, especially considering the age difference, but—"

"I'm almost thirty," I reminded him. "It's not like I'm in such a different place in my life than he is."

"Never thought I'd see the day our jet-setting sister settled down. For a while there, I thought you were content just fluttering around, leaving broken hearts in your wake."

My cheeks warmed. "I don't know if I'd say *broken*..."

"I know what you mean, though," Hunter told me. "For the longest time, I'd resigned myself that I was better off alone. Seeing what I did daily working in the hospital, I'd accepted being alone forever. And then..."

"And then, you fell in love with my wife's best friend?"

He chuckled. "Something like that. But it's just like you said. It just happened. Hit me like a million bricks, honestly. Suddenly, all I could think about was her. How to make her smile. What made her happy. What all of her favorite things were and how I could surprise her." He ran his fingers through his brown hair, a few shades lighter than mine, but somehow already streaked with a bit of gray.

I'd always liked that I looked a little like both of my brothers, like I'd gotten the best of both of them.

"I knew from the first moment I'd met Angelina," Benjamin said with a shrug. "I just had to convince her we'd be good together." He grinned. "And look at us now." He looked backwards into the kitchen, eyes filling with love, and I knew he was looking at his wife. "It's hard work; there's no doubt about it. But love is worth it."

I threw my arms around them both. "I love you guys. You're the best brothers I could have ever asked for."

"Come on, you two," Hunter said when we finally pulled apart. "It's getting cold. Let's go inside and open presents with the rest of our family."

Our family. A warmth spread through me, because for the first time, Mason was included in that too. For the first time, I wasn't the single sister with no significant other.

I grinned, and then let out a cackle. "I'm apologizing in advance for the presents I bought your children," I told them.

Kids' toys were *adorable*, and I'd gone all out. As the only aunt —since both Angelina and Gabbi only had brothers—I was trying to secure my status as the *cool aunt*. "Actually, you know, I'm not sorry."

We all laughed as we headed inside, back to the house that was filled with more love and laughter than it felt like it ever had been.

And all I could think was *yes*, I want more of this. More laughter, more love, more life. I wanted another tiny pair of feet running around here, but this pair belonging to Mason and me.

I wanted to put in the work, and I wanted to thank God for giving me this man every single day.

So that's what I was going to do.

One day at a time.

17

mason

I was in a staring contest with Hunter and Benjamin's wives, and I *really* wasn't sure what was going on. I'd never had a sister—maybe this is what it was like.

Both women were downright terrifying.

After Emily had slipped out of bed, I'd gotten up and come to the kitchen, starting breakfast for the whole family. Even though I'd known Hunter and Benjamin my entire life—and had considered the Sullivans like a second family—I wanted to impress them. I wanted them to see that I could be good for Emily, that I would take care of her and provide for her.

Even if she didn't need it, there was nothing I wouldn't do to prove that I was right for her. A year ago, I wasn't sure I'd ever be lucky enough to find someone again. To fall in love, to find someone who wanted all the same things as me. A life, marriage, a family.

But now it all felt in reach again. Craning my neck, I looked out the window.

My girl was outside, cuddled up under a blanket on the

back porch with her brothers. Hunter and Benjamin had nodded at me before heading out to join her, taking a seat on either side of the porch swing.

Pancakes were on the griddle when their wives had joined me downstairs, babies in tow. The twins looked like spitting images of Benjamin, dark hair with Angelina's brilliant blue eyes, while baby Quinlan was the perfect blend of both of her parents, brown hair pulled up into two tiny pigtails and a smattering of freckles on her cheeks.

God, I hoped our kids would be just as cute. It was way too early to be thinking about that, but I couldn't help but smile thinking about our conversation last night. Telling her I loved her had been incredible.

And knowing she loved me too? That she wanted the things I wanted?

That made the standoff I was currently in way easier to deal with.

"So… is one of you gonna say somethin', or is this just a stare-down until I break?" I raised an eyebrow at the two women. Honestly, they were downright terrifying when they wanted to be, especially ganging up on me.

They looked at each other, then back at me as I flipped another pancake. "Emily is like our little sister, you know," Angelina started, crossing her arms over her chest.

I nodded. Once upon a time, I would have said that too.

When had it stopped being true? Maybe when I'd met her again for the first time as an adult. She was such a strong, independent woman who seemed to sparkle wherever she went. Emily had traveled all over the world, sharing herself with hundreds of thousands of people online, and yet I'd never seen her have a bigger smile than when she was on top of her horse, riding through the Montana countryside covered in a fresh dusting of snow.

"I care about her," I told them, not wanting to hold back. "This isn't just some fling—not for either of us. It's real."

Angelina picked at her perfectly manicured red nails. I could almost imagine her sharpening them and using them as little tiny blades.

Gabbi gave me a soft smile. "You love her."

I ran my hand through my hair, looking out the window at her. "Yeah. I do. With all my heart and with all that I am. I wanna do right by her, you know? Give her everything she wants."

They both looked at each other, nodded, and then smiled at me. "Welcome to the family, Mason. We're glad Em seems to have found a good one. And we're happy to have you."

"Thank you." I cleared my throat, trying to hide the fact that I was a little choked up. I hadn't had a full conversation with Hunter yet—though that would come, as well as Em's parents once they were back from their tropical vacation—but just the idea of having their blessing meant the world to me. "I won't hurt her."

"No, you won't." A shudder ran down my spine at Angelina's intimidating glare. She was five-foot-ten, and I wasn't sure I'd ever seen her without her hair perfectly styled, heels, or a swipe of red lipstick on until this morning, when she'd come upstairs in a pair of Batman pajamas and her hair up in a messy ponytail. Still, she was still menacing, even if I had six inches and a lot of muscle on her.

Gabbi laughed. "Don't scare him off, Ang. We *like* this one, remember?" I was having a hard time believing her when she gave me a look that I was going to file away for later.

Right when I turned off the burner, a stack of pancakes ready to be devoured, the three Sullivan siblings all crowded inside, looking slightly misty-eyed but happy.

"You good?" I whispered into Em's ear as she walked over

to me, wrapping her arms around my stomach. I slid an arm around her shoulders, tugging her tight into my body.

"Never been better," she admitted.

I grinned. "That's what I like to hear, baby."

Kissing her on the forehead, I turned to everyone. "Merry Christmas, Sullivans. Who wants pancakes?"

one week later...

"That's the last of it," I said, carrying another box full of shoes into my cabin.

Emily looked up from a pile of clothes on the floor. "Thanks, cowboy."

"Of course," I told her. "Want me to help unpack?"

She bit her lip. "Are you sure?"

"Absolutely. This is your home now, too. Least I can do is help you."

As of today, she was officially moved in.

Over the last week, she'd been shuttling her stuff over, one bag at a time, like she thought I didn't know exactly what she was doing. As if I hadn't cleared out drawers for her the second I'd got back from her house on Christmas Day.

Today, I'd finally said, *enough.* After I'd finished my work on the ranch, we'd gotten in my truck, finished emptying her basement room, and I'd carried it all into the cabin. Now, her clothes hung side by side with mine in the closet. And she'd filled up the second one, too, with the rest—and her shoes, because my girl had more clothes than I was pretty sure I'd ever know what to do with.

Not that I was going to complain. I'd let her fill up my entire house with her things, because her presence made me feel whole. Like I'd been walking around with something missing for all these years, and I'd finally found it in the little vixen of a brunette.

God, I loved her so much.

So did my parents. The first night I'd brought her home for dinner—the day after Christmas—they'd spent the entire night talking to her, barely letting me get a word in edgewise. After we'd eaten, my mom had pulled out the old photo albums, finding the ones of us when we were little.

My favorite were the ones of little Emmie Girl in her pink cowgirl boots and pink hat.

She'd worn the one I'd given her that night, and it made my heart feel like it was fit to burst. What would she think if she knew the thoughts that were running through my head?

I fully intended to put a ring on her finger by the end of spring.

Was that too soon? I didn't think so. When my parents had gotten engaged, they'd been dating for two months. My dad told me he knew my mom was the one on their very first date. And look at them now. Happily married for thirty-eight years and still running the ranch together. Honestly, it felt like they were more in love with each other now than ever before.

And I'd had the same feeling with Emily. On the first night at the bar, I'd tried to downplay the connection I felt to her. I'd tried to ignore it, for my friendship with Hunter's sake, but I hadn't been able to.

Though, apparently, we owed some of our relationship to our meddling moms, too. Neither of them was as sly as they thought they were, however. When Em's mom had gotten back from her vacation, she'd let it slip that they'd been talking the whole time, scheming about ways to get us together.

Apparently, both of them thought we needed a little nudge because we were *lonely*. They were right, of course. My mom sending me over to check on Emily during that snow-storm had been the best thing that had ever happened for us.

And now, here we were—starting off the new year with her moving into my cozy little A-frame cabin. Starting the rest of our lives off *right*. It was small, but it was more than enough space for just the two of us.

I was already thinking about how I could expand it, though. I'd also been scouting areas on our property, thinking about building a big house with a wraparound porch. Enough bedrooms for as many kids as she wanted.

Getting ahead of myself? Maybe.

Her stomach rumbled, and I furrowed my eyebrows. I hadn't even thought of what I was going to feed her yet. But clearly, that was a problem I needed to fix, and quickly.

"What are you feeling for dinner tonight?" I asked her, leaning against the doorframe as I watched her put away a pair of dusty blue suede cowboy boots.

"Mmm." She bit her lip as she closed the closet. "What about breakfast? I've been dreaming about those pancakes you made on Christmas morning like every day since."

I laughed. "Sure, baby. I can do breakfast."

She stood up, wrapping her arms around my neck. "How did I get so lucky to find you? A hot cowboy who caters to my every whim?"

"I was thinkin' the same thing, darlin'." I smirked. "You're too damn good for me." I leaned down, pressing a kiss on her lips. "Gotta keep my girl satisfied."

Emily licked her lips. "*Satisfied*, huh?" She wiggled her eyebrows.

I dipped my lips to her ear. "Insatiable."

"Only for you," she confirmed.

I lifted her up into my arms, carrying her into the kitchen and setting her down on the marble countertop before kneeling in front of her. "Guess it's time for my dinner first, baby." Sliding my hands up her thighs, I pulled down her panties.

"Mason," she giggled, but the sound quickly turned into a moan with the first swipe of my tongue. "*Oh,* Mason." She was already wet for me, her arousal practically dripping out of her.

I grinned. "That's the sound I want to hear. Now come for me, darlin'. Give me that sweet release, and then I'll feed you anything you want."

And then I went to town on her. *Feasted,* savoring her taste with each lick, making her scream out my name before I finally made good on my word and cooked her the best damn breakfast she'd ever had.

Her cheeks were flushed when she took the first bite of her chocolate-chip pancakes.

"Good?" I asked, not taking a bite of my own yet.

"The best," she confirmed, letting out a happy sigh. "Thank you."

Leaning over, I dropped my head to hers, kissing her lazily and tasting the syrup on her tongue. "Don't have to thank me, Em. You've got me now. All of me. I told you I'm going to keep you satisfied." I winked, taking a few bites of food before reaching over and wiping a drip of syrup off her lip. "And I keep my promises."

"I know you do, cowboy." She climbed into my lap, running her thumb across my jaw. "That's one of the reasons I fell in love with you."

She kissed me—the rest of our food forgotten—and I picked her up in my arms, carrying her into the bedroom.

Our bedroom.

Where she'd stay for the rest of our lives, if I had anything to say about it.

"I love you," I told her as I stripped our clothes off. "So damn much, darlin'. Thank you for choosing me. For loving me. For seeing past the broken shell I used to be. I'm so grateful to call you mine." I kissed her bare skin.

Her hands slid into my hair, raking softly against my scalp. "I love you too, Mason Elliott. Now, make me yours." Her eyelashes fluttered as she widened her legs, cradling my hips between her thighs.

And because I'd never been able to say no to this girl—not once in my entire life—I slid inside of her, the feeling of *home* washing around me, and nothing else mattered.

Nothing but Emily Sullivan and this all-consuming love I felt for her. Nothing but the girl who had changed my entire life for the better in just a few weeks.

Better than any Christmas present I'd ever received.

"You are," I told her, thrusting inside of her in slow, languid strokes. "You're mine. All mine. Forever and ever."

She let her eyes flutter shut as I wrapped her in my arms, planting myself deep inside of her, and then there were no more words.

We didn't need them.

Not anymore.

Not with a love like this.

epilogue

Mason

one year later...

The snow was falling around us, landing on Emily's eyelashes as I held her close to me, unable to look away from her sparkling green eyes. My thumb rubbed across her cheek as she gave me a soft smile.

She took my breath away, even now. Her light brown hair was loose around her shoulders with an elegant braid swooping the top half back, catching more snowflakes as they settled from the sky.

"You're so beautiful," I murmured, brushing a tendril of hair back behind her ear.

"Mason," she whispered, her cheeks and nose slightly pink from the cold. Her white dress sparkled against the backdrop of the trees. She reached up, adjusting the brim of my brand new black cowboy hat.

"Still can't believe you're mine, darlin'." I couldn't stop touching her. Couldn't keep my hands off her any time I was around her, but somehow, today it was even harder. Maybe because she looked so beautiful and I'd barely had five minutes alone with her yet. I pressed my lips against her ear. "Going to show you just how much tonight."

Her eyelids fluttered. "Can't wait, cowboy." Reaching up, she grabbed the hat off my head and placed it on her own.

"Em…" I warned her, already feeling my tux pants growing tight. "You know what they say." Oh, did she ever. We'd recreated that scene in the stables multiple times over the past year, and it never stopped being the hottest thing I'd ever seen.

She smirked, draping her arms over my shoulders. "If I wear the hat, I gotta ride my cowboy."

"You're a vixen," I groaned.

Emily grinned. "Can you believe it's been a year since we got snowed in together?"

What a year it had been. "Best year of my life," I murmured, rubbing my nose against hers.

"Me too."

We'd spent countless hours on the backs of our horses, riding side by side. Emily had taken to ranch life better than I ever imagined. In fact, she thrived on it. Sure, she'd never be a horse trainer or a breeder—but I didn't want her to be. My favorite moments were watching her help my mom around the kitchen, leaning against the doorframe and watching them giggle to themselves when they didn't realize I was there. And then there were the times I'd find her interacting with the guests, particularly the kids, telling them all about her riding lessons at Midnight Pines Ranch.

Even the ones who were the most scared of horses seemed excited to get on one after that.

She was… incredible. There were no other words for it.

I loved watching her create content and curate her accounts, too. Watching her put together outfits and seeing how much stuff brands sent her, hoping just for a chance to be featured on her page.

Her social media pages had changed, but her followers didn't seem to mind that her content had shifted from traveling to her new life. Our life together.

The first photo she'd posted of us, everyone had gone crazy—even though it had just been our feet. A *soft launch*, she'd explained to me. I didn't know what the fuck that meant, but the photo had been her boots nestled between mine. It was the spark that started the fire, little photos she shared with my face hidden until Em finally posted one of me kissing her cheek, cowboy hat on my head, a giant smile on her face.

Then, everyone had demanded to know more about how she found her *hot cowboy*. Her words—not mine. But more than that—they were all happy for us. So was the entire town, thank fucking God. I hadn't known what I'd do if people disapproved of us together, of the eight year difference between us. But they hadn't.

Thanks to Em's posts, we couldn't keep up with bookings at the ranch thanks to her tagging the location on her profile. Everyone wanted to come to visit and get a taste of this life.

Plenty of them hoping to find their own cowboys.

Unfortunately for them, this cowboy was locked down tight. Had been since that day in the bar where I'd walked in and found the love of my life standing at it.

No regrets. I'd do it all over again if I had to, just to get right back here to the same position. My ring on her finger, glittering in the light just like the snow did.

I'd proposed in late spring, just like I'd planned, when the wildflowers had popped up and the meadow was full of them. That was where I'd gotten down on one knee and asked her to spend the rest of our lives together.

Thank fuck she'd said *yes*.

"I love you." I kissed her brow, and then her lips before stealing my hat back.

Emily adjusted her hands around my neck, letting one rest on my shoulder as the other still held a bouquet of white roses, her beautiful emerald green eyes matching the pine trees behind her. God, she was a miracle to behold. A wonder I still could barely fathom.

And she was mine.

A shutter clicked. "Got it!" The photographer announced. "You two are naturals."

"Hear that, baby?" I smirked. "A *natural.*"

She groaned, dropping her forehead against my tux.

And because I couldn't resist, I kissed my wife.

Wife.

Today was our wedding day. And while the rest of our families were sitting inside, out of the cold, we were the two crazy people taking photos in the snow.

But I wouldn't have it any other way.

"You're insufferable."

I grinned. "You married me, remember?" I held up my hand, showing off my titanium wedding band. "You're mine now, wife." She giggled as I kissed her ring, happiness shining off her face brighter than any sun.

"I think I've got everything photo-wise," Ava, our photographer, said, slipping her equipment back into her camera bag. "Unless there's anything else or any other poses you'd like?"

We'd probably taken hundreds of different photos—all sorts of angles and poses and backgrounds. But the snow really was beautiful. And my wife was resplendent.

No, she was positively *glowing.*

Emily looked up at me, biting her lip. "Do you still want to…?" Her question trailed off, but I knew exactly what she was thinking of. We'd talked about this moment for months.

How we'd tell our families. We wouldn't be able to hide it for much longer, after all.

Grinning, I let my hand rest over her stomach. You couldn't tell thanks to her dress, but her bump was there.

"The sonogram is in my pocket," I whispered in her ear.

We hadn't exactly planned on it when it happened, but one or two missed pills this summer had turned into two pink lines—and we'd both been ecstatic. And now, our baby was growing inside of her.

"One more photo, Ava?" Emily asked the photographer, sliding her hand into the interior pocket of my tux jacket, pulling out the small black-and-white photo.

She let out a small gasp. "Oh." She looked back and forth between the two of us. "You're...?"

My wife nodded. "Yeah." Her green eyes beamed up at me. "I'm four months along."

Pregnant. Emily was pregnant with our baby. Some days, I still couldn't believe it. Couldn't believe what a blessing this was, after everything I'd been through to get here. That after all this time, I was getting the future I'd always dreamed of. With the girl who was everything I could have ever asked for —and more. My soulmate. The love of my life.

Ava helped pose us—one of Em holding the sonogram over my shoulder, showing off her ring and the scan, with us wrapped up in each other. Another with me holding her bump, my hands cradling the little life growing inside of her.

"These photos are so perfect," she told us after taking one of me kissing Emily's belly. "Gosh, y'all are just going to have the most beautiful baby." Ava was originally from the south, and she'd just moved up to the area this past summer. Of course, she and Emily had been fast friends.

Tears pricked at Em's eyes. "Thank you." She looked over at me. "We haven't told anyone yet, though." Once we got back from our honeymoon, we were telling them all the good news. The photos were just a part of that. And our small way of having our baby be a part of our wedding day.

"My lips are sealed," she promised.

"I'm pretty sure some of them suspect, though," I said, laughing as I tugged her to my side. "Your brothers kept giving me weird looks last night when I kept finishing all of your drinks." And I could only slip her so much sparkling apple cider before I was pretty sure someone was going to catch on.

"The girls too," Emily admitted. "They're *all* getting a little too suspicious. It probably doesn't help that I threw up the night of the bachelorette party." She winced. "Not my finest moment."

Rubbing her back as we headed back towards the main lodge, I couldn't help but think of the memory of her crawling into our bed that night. The first trimester had been hard on her, and I'd done everything I could to help make it better. To take care of her, just like I promised.

We'd decided to get married on the ranch, the place we both loved. Of course, it had snowed the night before our wedding, and we trudged through the powdery layer of snow that had settled, turning the place into the perfect winter wonderland. Just like it had been during the storm that changed our lives forever.

"We'll tell them when we get back," I reminded her. This year, it was our turn to spend a magical two weeks in a tropical paradise. Even if the only pineapple drinks we'd be having were alcohol *free.*

She rested her hand on her bump, cradling our baby. "Yeah." A smile curled over her lips. "They're going to freak. I can't wait to tell your mom she's going to be a *grandma.*"

My mom was going to lose it. I had no doubt about that.

"There you two are," Jonah said as we approached the lodge, ready to slip back inside the cozy warmth. We were having the reception inside, though it had been completely redecorated for the occasion. The ceremony had been outside, under a trellis, with the only backdrop being the Montana forests and white winter snow. "Thought we'd lost you."

He was one of my groomsmen, along with Benjamin, plus Hunter as my best man. Emily's best friend Hannah had been her matron of honor, with her sisters-in-law as her bridesmaids.

My sisters-in-law now, as well. It felt crazy to think about that. In such a short time, I'd gone from being an only child to having this entire family. The guys I'd grown up with were now my brothers. Part of me still couldn't believe this was my life. We'd spent a lot of time with Hannah, her husband Tony, and their son Brandon over the last year, and it made me even more excited about welcoming our own child into the world next year.

"Sorry," Ava said, dipping her head as she blushed. "We wanted to grab a few more photos."

I couldn't help but notice there were sparks flying between my friend and our photographer. Huh. I filed that away in my memory to bring up to Emily later. If our parents had meddled in our love life, who was to say we couldn't help our friends also find happiness?

"Now, Mrs. Elliott." I turned to face my wife, holding out my hand to her. "I believe it's time for us to make our grand entrance."

Her answering smile was enough to warm me from the inside out, to not care that we'd been standing in the snow for the last few hours. "Okay, Mr. Elliott." She took my hand, and I kissed her softly before leading her into the room filled with our friends and family—filled with all the love we'd ever need in our lives—and sent a giant thank you up to the universe.

A year ago, I'd been alone. Still reeling from the divorce,

with my entire future pulled out from underneath me like a rug. Now, I was married again—this time, to the love of my life—and we were expecting our first child in the spring.

All because of a snowstorm. A snowstorm that made me see how good we could be together. That I couldn't deny the truth in front of me any longer. That this girl—this beautiful, incredible, awe-inspiring girl—was supposed to be mine.

I'd never squander that, or this opportunity to love her every day for the rest of our lives.

"You're mine," I whispered in her ear as we walked into the room to applause and cheers. Family and friends alike all so happy for us. "You and our baby. Forever and ever."

She looked up at me, tears dotting her eyelashes, and I pressed a kiss to her forehead.

This was the start of our forever, and I couldn't imagine it any other way.

Want to go back and see Emily's brothers fall in love? Read Disrespectfully Yours, Angelina and Benjamin's hate-to-love, workplace romance, friends with benefits story, and Fearlessly Yours, Gabbi and Hunter's best man x maid of honor, friends to lovers, vacation romance, both part of the **Best Friends Book Club** series, on kindle unlimited today!

extended epilogue

Emily

"**J**ust look at how cute they are, Han," I said to my best friend, holding up the *tiniest* pair of boots I'd ever seen. "They're so adorable I *literally* want to cry."

She shot me a look. "Please, for the love of all things good, do not cry over a pair of baby boots, Em."

"I can't help it." I pouted, sticking out my lower lip. "It's the hormones."

I was approximately the size of a house, eight months pregnant and still a month to go. My baby shower was yesterday, and when I'd woken up today, I'd decided that I needed to get all the gifts put away. The first thing I'd done was call my best friend for moral support while Mason was out working the horses. Luckily, she'd been able to sneak away, leaving Anthony with their almost two-year-old son.

Hannah rubbed my back, letting out a small sigh. "I remember that feeling when I was pregnant with Brandon."

I shook my head. "It's crazy. I never expected to be this happy, and I just…" There was no holding back my grin. "God, I just can't wait for her to be here, you know?"

The tiny pair of pink cowgirl boots from my sister-in-law Angelina were probably the cutest things I'd ever seen. Never mind that babies didn't need shoes or boots, because they couldn't even walk. I was never getting rid of them—ever.

Was this what Mason thought I was like with my own clothes? Okay, I probably was, but I was about to be so much worse. Tiny baby clothes were my kryptonite. I'd never cried over something so small before. Had never stared at so many little bitty outfits in stores, even when I'd been shopping for my niece and nephews.

Our baby was about to be the best-dressed kid Midnight Pines Ranch had ever seen.

"Emily."

I blinked. "Huh?" I'd totally zoned out on her.

She laughed. "Are you actually crying?"

"Shut up," I groaned, dabbing at my eyes before looking over at my best friend. "I'm going to be a monster, aren't I?"

She nodded. "Absolutely. But all the best moms are."

A mom. I still couldn't believe I was going to be someone's mom. My eyes watered, and my best friend took the shoes from me, setting them down on the counter as I rubbed at my belly, feeling baby girl kick.

In a month, she'd be here, in our arms. *Finally.*

I couldn't wait to meet our little girl. I couldn't wait. My wedding ring sparkled on my left hand, catching the light. How was it possible that I was this happy?

Laughing, I shook my head. "Most moms don't have to clear out the second bedroom that they were using as a closet to make room for their baby."

"Nope, babe. Just you." She winked at me. "But my closet was very grateful for the new clothes." Hannah gestured to her top, something I'd purged a few months back when I decided some of it had to go. I'd amassed a huge amount of clothes with all the different brand partnerships and collaborations I'd done over the years.

"It looks better on you than it ever did on me," I admitted, only slightly annoyed that my best friend had the perfect figure—and that she could bend over without a giant basketball-sized belly in the way. "Not that they fit anymore, anyway," I pouted.

Hannah rolled her eyes. "Stop. You're gorgeous."

"God, I'm ready to evict this girl. She's been sitting on my bladder for way too long. Speaking of…"

Hannah laughed. "Go. I'll finish putting these away." She gestured to the pile of clean onesies and outfits that were piled on top of the dresser.

"Are you sure?" I bit my lip. "I can do it later…"

She shook her head, giving me a small smile. "Go. I got this, babe."

"I don't deserve you," I said, sighing.

Heading to the bathroom—not quickly, because I never did anything fast these days—I trudged back in a few minutes later, finding the room much cleaner than when I'd left it.

"You're a miracle worker."

"Anything for my best friend." She winked.

I rubbed my back. "Mason and I keep meaning to come in and finish everything in here, but it's so busy on the ranch with foaling season…"

Besides helping make sure everything was going well with the guests on the ranch, Mason also had his hands in helping with the births of the foals, getting a call when the mares were about to deliver.

I'd tried to ignore the fact that it was going to be *me* pushing an eight plus pound baby out of me soon. Ouch.

"God, right? Tony's been working extra long hours with the

cattle. He's up before the sun most days. I just want to stay in bed with my husband." She winked. "Especially before B wakes up. We need some alone time, if you know what I mean."

Humming, I picked up a baby blanket, picking at a loose thread. "Do you miss it?" I asked, looking around at the piles of gifts. "All this?" The nursery was an explosion of pink and ruffles and lace. Mason and I were having a girl. I'd never forget the way he'd cried when they'd told us the gender, or how he'd teared up when he'd seen our baby on the ultrasound for the first time.

Ever since we'd found out I was pregnant, he had seemed happier than ever. And I knew it wasn't just about the baby; it was about the family we were making.

He was home early every night to make dinner, to talk with me about the future, about all of his hopes and dreams for the little human we had created. And God, I'd dreamed of this, too, but I'd never imagined it would feel like this.

Hannah smiled. "That snuggly baby stage…" She let out a deep sigh. My best friend squeezed my arm. "You'll see soon. And, well…" She grinned. "Might not miss it for too much longer if you know what I mean."

"Ohmygod," I squealed. "Han. Are you—?"

My best friend nodded. "We'd been talking about it a *lot*, and well…" She dropped her hand to her abdomen. "We just found out, so we didn't want to tell anyone yet. Both of us grew up with siblings, and I don't want to wait too long to give Bran a sibling. He's already almost two."

I nodded, holding the pink baby blanket to my chest. "I already know I want more. Growing up with Hunt and Ben, even though they were a lot older than me, I can't imagine not having them."

"Bet it doesn't hurt that you fell in love with your older brother's best friend, either." Hannah snorted.

Laughing, I just shook my head at her as I heard the tell-tale noise of the front door of our cabin opening and closing.

"Darlin'?" came Mason's voice.

"In here!" I announced, feeling a flutter in my chest at the sound of my cowboy's voice. Just like always. Our daughter kicked right on time—as if she knew he was home, too—and I placed my hand over the spot.

I loved my man—and I loved how much he loved the ranch—but I didn't trust myself around him right now. Especially when he walked in here wearing that damn hat on his head. It was like my catnip. There was no way I could resist him, not when he was all hot, sweaty, and cowboy'd up.

He appeared in the doorway, looking handsome as ever with his dark beard trimmed close to his face and those beautiful blue eyes I loved shining at me. "There's my girl." Mason crossed the room in the time it took me to blink, pressing his lips to my cheeks. "Hi, Hannah."

She smiled at my husband. "How's it going, Mason?"

"Better now," he answered, wrapping his arms around me and swaying me softly.

"I should get home," Hannah said, laughing. "God knows Tony is probably waiting for me."

"Thanks for keeping me company." I waddled over to her, wrapping my arms around her. "I love you." She wasn't the biggest hugger, but she wrapped her arms around me, anyway.

"Love you too, Em." She pulled away and then looked at my husband. "Don't let her be in here too long. She almost cried over boots earlier."

Mason raised an eyebrow. "Again?"

I crossed my arms over my chest, resting them on top of my bump. "I can't help it. They're so small."

He chuckled as Hannah slipped outside, leaving us alone in the nursery. "How are you feeling?"

I bit my lip. *"Giant.* Exhausted." I looked him up and down. "Horny."

He took a few steps towards me. "Horny, huh?"

I nodded, taking a step backwards for each of his approaching movements until my back hit the wall. "Uh-huh."

His tongue clicked against the roof of his mouth. "Well, we can't have that, can we, *darlin'*?" The way he dragged out the nickname felt like a rasp against my skin. I shivered. He stepped in front of me, his nose brushing up my neck.

"Mason." The whine slipped out of my throat. "I want you."

He brushed my hair back from my face, kissing each of my cheeks softly as his hands cupped the swell of my belly. "Look at you. My pretty little wife, carrying my baby, begging me so sweetly."

I let out a soft whimper as he pulled my dress up, exposing my lacy underwear. He dropped to his knees, kissing the insides of my thighs, running his nose over the lace fabric like he was inhaling my scent. Like he couldn't get enough of me.

"Fuck," he muttered, groaning as he ran his tongue over the fabric before sucking my clit into his mouth—underwear and all. "Soaked for me, huh, baby?"

"Yes," I agreed, letting my head rest against the wall as he continued his ministrations. No matter what he did, it felt so damn good. It didn't hurt that I was so keyed up, just from seeing him all sweaty in his hat.

He stood up to his full height, towering over me, and I flicked the brim of his hat up as he leaned his head towards mine, lips brushing my lips. "Gonna have to take care of my darlin' wife," he murmured against my mouth before looping his arms around my body and picking me up.

"Mason," I protested, knowing my body wasn't the same

as it had been when we first met. "You don't have to carry me."

"If I can't carry my pregnant wife, what good is all the work I do on my body?" He winked at me—actually winked —and my panties flooded with arousal.

Yeah, I was *soaked.*

"Not fair," I pouted as he carried me into our bedroom, setting me down on the bed. "You're so hot, and I look like this." I waved a hand over my body as he undid his belt buckle.

Mason frowned. "Like what?"

"You know…" I bit my lip. "Huge."

"Darlin'." His deep rasp made my nipples stand at attention. "If I haven't done enough to show you I fuckin' love your body like this, that's my fault. But I think it's sexy as hell watching you grow our baby. Seeing your body swell and knowing *I'm* the one who did that to you. Kinda makes me wanna do it all over again after this one." He took his hat off, setting it on my head before grabbing my hand, placing it over the hardened bulge in his pants. "Feel that?" He asked. "Feel what you do to me?"

I nodded, feeling a little breathless as I squeezed his cock, already desperate to have it inside of me. "I just—"

"No buts." He sank down to the floor, kneeling in front of me. "Apparently I've gotta show you just how damn much I like it. How much I *love* this body." He spread my knees apart, pulled my dress off, and hooked his fingers into my panties before tugging. "Lift your hips, Em."

I complied—because what else did you do when your hot cowboy husband was on his knees in front of you, telling you how attractive he found you—and let him pull my under-wear off my body until I was bare to him. He flattened his tongue, licking up my entrance before circling my clit once, twice, three times. His fingers dug into my thighs as he kept me spread for him, lick after glorious, torturous lick over my pussy, tasting me but not giving me enough friction to come —not giving me what I needed.

He groaned as he plunged his tongue into my wet heat, lapping up my arousal. One perk of pregnancy was my heightened sensitivity and arousal. It was hard not to want him *all the damn time.*

"Mason." I thrust my fingers into his hair, forcing him deeper. He kept up eating me out until I was practically crying, bucking my hips and trying to grind against him, needing more, more, *more.*

I shut my eyes, feeling my orgasm build, the peak getting closer and closer and—Mason stopped. He stood up, hands resting on his belt buckle as his eyes slowly swept up and down my body.

"Look at you," he praised. "So beautiful. And all mine."

Suddenly, all I wanted was to tear his clothes off him. I reached my hands out towards his pants, and he clicked his tongue against the roof of his mouth, stilling me.

"Do you trust me?"

I nodded. "Always." I always had. Ever since I was a little girl, I'd trusted him. Loved him. It was different now—it had been different since that day in the bar. Since we'd gotten snowed into my parent's house together. And yet, I would always feel this way. I knew it deep in my soul. He was the only one for me. The love of my life. My cowboy.

He rested his forehead against mine. "Then you'll trust me to know what you need. That I'll take care of you." My husband pressed a kiss to my forehead.

"Yes," I agreed. Because I knew he would take care of my body, just like he did my heart. Ever since I'd found out I was pregnant, it was even clearer just how much he worshipped me, body and soul.

He made a satisfied sound. "Good. Because you know

what they say." His eyes ran over my body like a gentle caress. "If you wear the hat, you gotta ride the cowboy." He pulled his belt off before letting it fall to the ground with a loud thud. Mason's pants came next, as he kicked them off, revealing his black boxer briefs that left nothing to the imagination. Not that I needed to imagine it anymore.

After ridding himself of his shirt, Mason climbed onto the bed, lying back against the pillows before sliding his hand up my thigh. "Come on, baby. Ride me."

I straddled his hips, pinning his cock between us as I planted my hands on his chest, running my fingers through his chest hair. Mason was still the sexiest man I'd ever seen, tall and built like a *man*, with muscles that I never failed to ogle. Because damn, if you had a man that looked like that, why would you ever look anywhere else?

"God, baby." He slid his hands up my bump, caressing the spot where our baby grew inside me. "I can't get over how gorgeous you are like this."

I let my eyes drift shut, rocking my hips in slow motion back and forth as I enjoyed the feeling of his hands on my skin—the gentle exploration that always felt like *more*. It was full of love and devotion, as his fingers brushed over every inch of my body, tracing my curves until they found my lacy bra. "Let me see those tits, baby."

Eager to comply, I reached up, unhooking it in the back and shimmying out of the straps. I'd had to buy a whole new slew of lingerie thanks to how much they'd grown during pregnancy, but the way Mason's eyes darkened and his breath caught, I knew it was worth it.

"Fuck me." He cupped both breasts with his calloused hands, squeezing lightly, brushing the pads of his thumbs over my nipples. I let out a moan as he pinched them, sensations running through my body. "I love these. So sensitive now."

I gasped, grinding down against his length as he squeezed again. "Need you," I begged, rubbing harder, faster, each rock of my hips providing delicious stimulation for my poor, needy clit.

Mason groaned, gripping my hips and guiding me up to allow me to position his head at my entrance before sinking back down on him. Both of us let out a low moan of satisfaction as he filled me, inch by glorious inch.

I didn't move—not at first, needing the time for my body to get used to the fullness of his large cock entering me. And then, when it was clear neither of us could take it anymore, I rocked my hips, the movement bringing sweet, sweet relief.

"That's my cowgirl," he praised. "Ridin' me so fuckin' good, baby. Looking like a goddamn miracle in my hat. How'd I get so lucky?" He squeezed my thighs as I moved in earnest, rolling my hips over and over and over, chasing the orgasm my body had been craving. "Take what you need. It's all yours, anyway. Always has been."

It didn't take much more for me to come as we worked in tandem—Mason thrusting his hips up, bringing his thumb to my clit and applying pressure—and then I was crying out his name, practically flying, the feeling even better than when I was on the back of a horse, the fresh Montana air whipping through my hair. A feeling I hadn't gotten to experience recently, because I was banned from that kind of riding for now.

At least I still had my favorite ride. I'd save as many horses as needed to ride this cowboy. *Yeehaw*.

My pussy was still spasming around Mason's length, my body coming down from the high of my orgasm, when I felt his hard-as-steel length twitching inside of me.

"Em," he groaned, each thrust of his hips inside of me bringing him closer. He was so close, I could *feel* it. "Going to fill you up," he promised. "Keep you all soft and round for me, huh, baby?"

"Yes," I whimpered, dropping my head back, not caring that the hat fell off my head as I cupped my breasts, needing something, needing *more*—

And then, with a grunt, he came, spilling inside of me, pumping me full of his cum with every thrust, and all I could do was take it, take this beautiful man's everything, because he was all I wanted, and *this* was all I wanted. All I needed, really. A family with the cowboy who meant everything. A future with the man who'd already given me everything.

With our breathing still rough, I collapsed against his chest, his softening cock still buried deep inside of me. He wrapped his arms around my back, my bump the only thing keeping us from being pressed tightly together. I ran my fingers through his hair, pressing my lips to his neck and trailing soft kisses all across his collarbone. We were both sated and well spent, and now, all I wanted was to have him hold me, just like this.

"You're the best thing that ever happened to me," he murmured as he rolled us onto our sides, cradling my belly like he always did after sex. "Fuck, but I love you, darlin'."

I smiled. "I love you too, cowboy. Thanks for being mine."

Forever and always.

He pressed a kiss to my lips. "No one else's I'd rather be."

And I knew that was the truth—that even if we had to do it all over again, we'd still be here, in the most gorgeous house on his family's horse ranch, living the best life I could have ever pictured for myself.

That was how it was going to be for the rest of time, because he was my happy ending. He was my soulmate, if that was a thing, and I was so damn grateful for every moment with him.

"Did you mean what you said?" I asked, letting out a small laugh. "About more kids?"

His eyes sparkled with mischief. "As soon as I can, Em, I'm knocking you up again."

I let out a small hum. "Just checking."

Turns out I liked the sound of that.

But maybe it was just him, and *us*.

That I liked anything that had to do with Mason Elliott and this life we'd built together.

My brother's childhood best friend.

My cowboy.

My husband.

My love of my life.

My happy ending.

The End.

acknowledgments

To my readers: thank you!! I wouldn't be here without you, truly. I appreciate every single post, graphic, and every one of you who continues to share about my books.

To Cat, Hannah, Olivia: thank you for being my besties and always supporting me & having my back. You're the best.

To Meagan: I love you so much and am so glad to have you in my life. Can't wait to stare at hockey & cowboy butts with you soon.

To my author friends (you know who you are): thank you for your never-ending support, encouragement, and love. There's not enough words in the English language to describe how grateful I am to have such amazing friends in my corner.

To my family: thank you for being my biggest supporters and cheerleaders. I don't know how I got so lucky.

also by jennifer chipman

contemporary romance

Best Friends Book Club

Academically Yours - Noelle & Matthew

Disrespectfully Yours - Angelina & Benjamin

Fearlessly Yours - Gabrielle & Hunter

Gracefully Yours - Charlotte & Daniel

Merrily Mine - Emily & Mason

Famously Mine - Tessa & Oliver (coming 2026)

Cousins Coffee Club

(Best Friends Book Club Generation 2)

Uniquely in Love - Ellie & Owen

Wildly in Love - Quinlan & Sawyer (coming summer 2026)

Castleton University

A Not-So Prince Charming - Ella & Cameron

Once Upon A Fake Date - Audrey & Parker

A North Pole Christmas

Elfemies to Lovers - Ivy & Teddy

paranormal romance

Witches of Pleasant Grove

Spookily Yours - Willow & Damien

Wickedly Yours - Luna & Zain

Bewitchingly Hers - Eryne & Barrett

Eternally His - Rina & Ezra (coming fall 2026)

Hauntingly Hers - Wendy & Cassius (coming winter 2026)

science fiction romance

S.S. Paradise

A Love Beyond the Stars - Aurelia & Sylas

about the author

Originally from the Portland area, Jennifer now lives in Orlando with her dog, Walter and cat, Max. In her free time, you can find her with her nose in a book or going to the Disney Parks. She loves writing romance heroes who fall first and hard for their women. Jennifer writes Contemporary Romance, Paranormal Romance, and Sci-Fi Romance.

Website: www.jennchipman.com

amazon.com/author/jenniferchipman

goodreads.com/jennchipman

instagram.com/jennchipmanauthor

facebook.com/jennchipmanauthor

x.com/jennchipman

tiktok.com/@jennchipman

pinterest.com/jennchipmanauthor

www.ingramcontent.com/pod-product-compliance
Lightning Source LLC
Chambersburg PA
CBHW060449300726
48975CB00008B/2452